Brooke nearly jumped when Ryan placed his plate in the sink.

"Thanks again for breakfast."

He was so close, she'd swear his breath caressed her cheek, a manly scent of the outdoors and honest work. It was headier than any cologne.

"You're welcome."

Brooke fought the crazy urge to turn slightly, to see just how close he was, what he might do. Before she had time to act on that thought, he was out the back door.

She closed her eyes, gripped the edge of the sink and exhaled. Then, unable to resist, she walked into the family dining room and watched as he headed back toward his slice of the ranch, doing more for a worn pair of jeans than any high-dollar model could ever dream of doing.

Brooke sighed, she was in trouble, and she wasn't sure she minded it one bit.

Dear Reader,

I believe it's impossible for a writer to not have her
own experiences color her stories. I know that each
one of mine is influenced by the things I've done, seen
and heard. *Cowboy to the Rescue* is no different. It takes
place in a fictional town, but Blue Falls sprang from
my imagination while I was traveling through the Texas
Hill Country. Its beauty is very different from that of
the verdant South where I have lived all my life, but I
think the difference is what attracts me. In the place
of green rolling hills, the Hill Country has fields of
wildflowers, cactus plants, views that go on for miles
and a rich ranching and German heritage. How could I
not be inspired by that?

Brooke, the heroine of *Cowboy to the Rescue*, has one
sibling, a sister, and two nieces. I have the same. And
like Brooke, I live several states away from them, so I
can write those feelings of missing them with some
authenticity. My sister and I share a lifelong love of
books, and we can often be found instant-messaging
each other with the question, "So, what are you
reading?" When this book hits store shelves, I know
what her answer better be.

I hope you enjoy Ryan and Brooke's story. I loved
writing this book, a story of two broken souls who
finally heal when they find each other. When I write
a book that can make me tear up, I know I'm doing
something right.

Trish Milburn

Cowboy to the Rescue

TRISH MILBURN

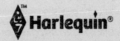
Harlequin®

TORONTO NEW YORK LONDON
AMSTERDAM PARIS SYDNEY HAMBURG
STOCKHOLM ATHENS TOKYO MILAN MADRID
PRAGUE WARSAW BUDAPEST AUCKLAND

Recycling programs
for this product may
not exist in your area.

ISBN-13: 978-0-373-75400-7

COWBOY TO THE RESCUE

Copyright © 2012 by Trish Milburn

ABOUT THE AUTHOR

Trish Milburn wrote her first book in the fifth grade and has the cardboard-and-fabric-bound, handwritten and colored-pencil-illustrated copy to prove it. That "book" was called *Land of the Misty Gems,* and not surprisingly it was a romance. She's always loved stories with happy endings, whether those stories come in the form of books, movies, TV programs or marriage to her own hero.

A print journalist by trade, she still does contract and freelance work in that field, balancing those duties with her dream-come-true career as a novelist. Before she published her first book, she was a finalist eight times in the prestigious Golden Heart contest sponsored by Romance Writers of America, winning twice. Other than reading, Trish enjoys traveling (by car or train—she's a terra firma girl!), watching TV and movies, hiking, nature photography and visiting national parks.

You can visit Trish online at www.trishmilburn.com. Readers also can write to her at P.O. Box 140875, Nashville, TN 37214-0875.

Books by Trish Milburn

HARLEQUIN AMERICAN ROMANCE

1228—A FIREFIGHTER IN THE FAMILY
1260—HER VERY OWN FAMILY
1300—THE FAMILY MAN
1326—ELLY: COWGIRL BRIDE
1386—THE COWBOY'S SECRET SON*

*The Teagues of Texas

To Mary. I love you, sis. (P.S. I found it. LOL!)

Chapter One

Brooke Vincent wiped her sweaty palms on her khaki slacks, hoping the woman sitting across from her didn't notice. She needed this job, but didn't want to appear as desperate as she actually was.

"You seem like a nice girl, but your résumé is a little thin," Merline Teague said as she sat back in her office chair.

Understatement of the year.

"I know," Brooke said. "I guess I've been one of those free spirits, trying to experience lots of different things." Brooke winced at the lie, at how it might make her seem like a bad bet to hire. Of all the untraceable things she'd put on her résumé, the only one that held any truth was the summer backpacking trip through Europe. It'd been an unexpected and fantastic gift from her mother before Brooke had gone to college, the first thing to really expose her to the wide and varied world outside of West Virginia.

"Well, there is something to be said for seeing a bit of the world and finding yourself while you're still young," Mrs. Teague said.

Brooke tried not to get her hopes up too high at the older woman's seeming understanding.

"Do you feel like your wandering days are over, at least for a while?" Mrs. Teague asked.

"Yes, ma'am." A little surge of hope swelled in Brooke, but she did her best to hide it.

The proprieter of the Vista Hills Guest Ranch rested her elbows on the arms of her chair and clasped her hands over her chest. "Being a cook for a guest ranch seems tame next to touring the Yorkshire moors and walking in the Brontë sisters' footsteps."

Brooke hurried to assure Mrs. Teague she wouldn't be disappointed in life in rural Texas. "Not really. Every place has its own personality," Brooke said. "Here, there seems to be a real connection to the land, a unique identity like you've stepped out of one world and into another."

When she noticed the surprised expression on her potential employer's face, Brooke nearly kicked herself. She sounded like a splashy tourist brochure. If she truly wanted to leave her old life behind and start over, she had to stop acting like a polished city dweller who was very good at reading people and telling them what they wanted to hear.

But that was the problem, wasn't it? She didn't really want to start over. Sometimes you just didn't have a choice.

She forced a laugh she was far from actually feeling. "Sorry. Guess I've been reading too many travel magazines. I just really enjoy cooking and believe I could do a good job for you." At least that much was true.

Mrs. Teague didn't immediately respond. Instead, she sat staring at Brooke as if she was dissecting every word Brooke had spoken, every facial expression and eye movement. It proved remarkably difficult not to fidget.

"I tell you what," Mrs. Teague finally said. "I'll give you a tryout. The guests are on their own tonight, so you can cook for the family. If it goes well, we'll talk again after dinner."

Brooke schooled her expression, cloaking an excitement she would have never imagined a year ago. "What would you like?"

Mrs. Teague smiled. "Surprise us."

Her mind jumped to all the elegant menus at the Davenport, the hotel where she'd been the convention manager, a parade of high-end entrées and decadent desserts. But this wasn't a four-star hotel in Washington, D.C. A guest ranch in the Hill Country of Texas required a bit different fare from Maine lobster and hazelnut soufflé.

"Okay. You won't be disappointed, Mrs. Teague. I promise."

Please let me fulfill that promise.

"Well, come on." Mrs. Teague stood and motioned for her to follow. "Let me show you the kitchen and dining areas. You can look through the supplies, see if you need to go into town for anything."

When they reached the kitchen, it was bigger and more modern than she expected. It occupied the back half of a great room that also included the family's comfortable-looking living area. A large dark-wood island stood in the center of the kitchen with copper-bottomed pots hanging from an iron rack overhead. Cobalt-blue and terra-cotta tiles covered the floor and backsplashes, and marble countertops gleamed. Her hands itched to put the stainless steel appliances to work creating something scrumptious. Amongst the appreciation was a pang for the kitchen she'd left behind, that entire life.

She shook off those negative thoughts and made herself focus on the tour.

Mrs. Teague pointed toward the dining room adjacent to the kitchen. "When it's just family, we eat in here. But when guests are here for meals, we use the dining area we added to the back of the house." She motioned for Brooke to follow her through a set of glass double doors on the back side of the kitchen.

The room she stepped into had the same feel as the other parts of the house she'd seen: homey, Western, welcoming. Several wooden tables were scattered around the room. Punched-tin napkin holders sat alongside salt and pepper shakers in the shapes of cowboy hats and boots. A long wooden sideboard with leather-covered front drawers and forged-iron drawer pulls occupied one wall. A mammoth antler chandelier hung from the middle of the ceiling.

"We have ten guest cabins, so we're set up here to feed up to forty people," Mrs. Teague said. "Though it's not often that many. Sometimes it's mainly couples, so the number might be half that. Then you have late sleepers who skip breakfast, and the tourists who want to try out the restaurants in town. But we ask the guests to give us a meal count each day for the next day so we know how many to cook for."

Brooke continued to scan the facilities. "It's a lovely room." More intimate than the hotel ballrooms she was used to.

"Thanks. We didn't want it to feel impersonal like a lot of places that serve large numbers all at once." With that, Mrs. Teague led the way back into the kitchen.

"That's about it," she said after she'd pointed out a few more highlights. "Any questions?"

Brooke shook her head. "I don't think so."

"Then let's shoot for six o'clock." She patted Brooke's hand where it sat palm down on the large, cool surface of the island.

The friendly, familiar gesture surprised Brooke. But based on her limited knowledge of the other woman, it seemed totally in character.

The phone rang, drawing Mrs. Teague's attention to the caller ID. "Oh, I'm sorry but I have to take this."

"Okay, no problem."

Brooke smiled as Mrs. Teague headed out of the room, hoping only a few more hours stood between her and a job. Because, honestly, if she didn't get this position, she didn't know if she had the energy to start her search over again. When she'd found the ad online for the ranch cook opening at Vista Hills, something had made her latch on to it, planning her new life around the idea of working here.

She hoped that decision proved wiser than the one that had led her to Texas. The one that had forced her to walk away from the person she'd been before, as if Brooke Alder had never existed.

RYAN TEAGUE PRESSED the hot brand into the board, the last piece of a large trunk he'd just finished constructing. When he pulled the branding iron away from the wood, his nose tingled as it always did from the scorched scent in the air.

He smoothed his hand over the image—a *VHR* flanked by a simple wildflower on one side and a horse on the other. He made a mental note to call the doctor in San Marcos who'd ordered the trunk as a wedding gift for his daughter.

After hanging the branding iron in its spot next to his shop's large outdoor stone fireplace, Ryan wiped the sweat from his face and headed inside to cool off and get a drink. It was only mid-May, but central Texas was already doing its damnedest to give Hades a run for its money in the heat race. Still, anything was better than the merciless inferno that was the Iraqi desert.

He froze halfway to the fridge as a chill swept through him, one that had nothing to do with the cranked air-conditioning. He closed his eyes, brought a view of the ocean to mind, and imagined the sound of the waves. He inhaled and exhaled slowly—once, twice, three times.

The moment passed, thank God not a true flashback this time. They were less frequent now than they'd been two years ago, when he'd been shipped home with a hole in his leg the size of a baseball.

As if the injury had happened yesterday, he felt that blinding pain again. He fought the urge to reach down and rub the side of his thigh. But the pain was all in his head, his memories. He hardly ever even limped anymore. Months and months of hard work had him walking normally so he didn't have to be reminded of that horrible day every time he put weight on his leg.

Harder to banish was a head full of images no one should ever have to see. Despite the therapy and his family's support, he still wasn't sure the lessening of the flashbacks was a good thing. Part of him still believed he deserved them.

With a curse, he shoved those thoughts back to the other side of the world and crossed the distance to the fridge. He jerked the door open and...found it empty.

He'd forgotten to restock. What a surprise. Sometimes he'd swear being nearly blown up had knocked some of his memory loose. As if to punish him for his absentmindedness, the sides of his parched throat stuck together. Time to go pilfer some sodas from his parents until he could get into town to buy his own. And with the length of the order list for his custom-made furniture, God only knew when that would be.

He walked the short distance from his shop-home combo to the main drive into the ranch. His parents' house, the ranch office and the horse barn were visible the moment he made the turn. Even though he didn't live far from his parents, a hill and several large live oak trees gave him the privacy he needed.

Choco, the family's chocolate Lab, descended the steps from the front porch and ambled out to meet him.

"Hey, boy," Ryan said as he crouched and gave the dog a good scratching between the ears. He nodded toward where Nacho, the yellow Lab, lay watching them from the porch. "I see your buddy is as lazy as ever."

Choco snorted as if agreeing. Ryan laughed then resumed his trek toward refreshment.

When he stepped in the back door to the kitchen, he noticed his mom standing behind the open refrigerator door.

"Perfect timing," he said. "Please tell me you have a cold 7-Up in there."

When the fridge examiner leaned back, it most definitely wasn't his mother. Instead, a dark-haired, dark-eyed beauty stared back at him.

"Oh, sorry. Thought you were my mom." For a moment he felt as though he'd wandered into the wrong house, then he thought maybe this woman was a guest. But why was she in the kitchen with no one else around?

Or had his mom finally hired a new cook? After years of seeing Trudy helping his mom in the kitchen, he hadn't been prepared for someone near his own age.

He hadn't even known his mom's weeks of interviews had finally come to an end.

"You're Mrs. Teague's son?" Was that a touch of nervousness in her voice?

"One of them. Ryan. Are you the new cook?"

The woman placed a package of chicken on the island and closed the fridge.

"Not yet. I'm making your parents dinner tonight, sort of a tryout."

A tryout? His mom hadn't required that of any of the other applicants. Then it clicked what day it was. He laughed, but at the stricken look on the woman's face he reined himself in.

"Sorry. Bit of a family joke." He pointed toward the calendar on the wall, one adorned with prints by famous Western painters like Frederic Remington and Charles Russell. "Thursday is family night around here, with mandatory attendance by all. We each take a turn providing the meal and entertainment. Guess whose night it is."

"Your mother's?"

"Bingo."

She smiled, just a little, but it was enough to make something in his chest perform an unexpected flip-flop.

Not a good thing.

He forced any hint of a smile from his expression and headed toward the refrigerator. Damn, he had to remember to buy his own drinks.

"I shouldn't have assumed I was just cooking for two," she said.

"Mom didn't tell you how many to cook for?" That was odd.

"She got a phone call she had to take when we were talking, and then headed over to the office. I guess she just forgot when she got busy, and I assumed when she said 'just the family,' she meant her and your father."

Ryan stared into the fridge, not seeing any 7-Up. He grabbed an orange soda instead and closed the door. When he turned around, she—whatever her name was—was eyeing the chicken and chewing on her lip.

"Seven adults, one six-year-old boy."

Her gaze met his, and for some reason he got the feeling that part of her was somewhere else. "Huh?"

"That's how many you're cooking for."

She exhaled as though she'd been holding her breath. "Oh, thanks. That helps."

They stared at each other until it grew awkward. She broke eye contact first, picking up a pen and pad from a basket on the island.

"Well, good luck," he said, then headed toward the back door that led outside.

"Thank you."

He nodded then hurried outside, overcome with the need for fresh air, to not be trapped in the kitchen with a nameless woman who'd caused his system to jump off its normal, everyday rails with one look of her big, brown eyes. Doe eyes.

After he stalked several yards away, he stopped and looked back at the house.

What had caused him to react to her that way? It certainly wasn't the first time he'd seen a beautiful woman. He couldn't remember ever fleeing from one before as if she was a giant spider on the verge of capturing him in a web.

Choco nuzzled his hand, looking for more affection. Ryan gave the dog what he wanted without even looking. The longer he stood in the middle of the driveway, the more realization sank in.

He was attracted to the mystery woman in his mother's kitchen. Really attracted. Other than panic and fear from his nightmares, he hadn't felt anything that strongly since he'd come home. And that frightened him more than facing armed insurgents.

BROOKE KEPT LISTING possible dishes to make for dinner, then crossing them off—too fancy, too country, too exotic, always too something. It didn't help that she kept glancing at the back door, wondering if Ryan Teague might reappear.

She shook her head and pressed her palm against her forehead. Daydreaming about a tall Texan with blue-green eyes so striking she'd momentarily forgotten how to speak wasn't going to help her get this job. Focusing on him instead of her task would probably ensure she didn't.

Another look at her list gave her an entirely new idea. Two menus. Two different menus to show her versatility.

Twice as much work.

But twice the opportunity to showcase her skills, and worth it if she secured the position.

She located and mixed ingredients for spiced pork chops with butternut squash, filet mignon with twice-baked potatoes, orange-juice cake and caramel brioche. And to cater to the child Ryan had mentioned, she whipped up some fancy cupcakes that, she had to admit, were almost too pretty to eat. As she arranged them on a serving tower, she wondered if the little boy was his.

Not important.

The minutes ticked ever closer to six o'clock, but she squeezed them for all they were worth. By the time she was done, she had enough food to feed a platoon of hungry stomachs.

Only when she stopped to take a breath did she realize no one had entered the kitchen since Ryan had left. And she felt she knew the Teagues' kitchen as well as the one she'd cooked in for the past year.

Now that the food was prepared and the table set, she had to make herself as presentable as she could in, oh, three minutes. She hurried to the bathroom located down the hall, smoothed her hair, dusted the flour off her red blouse, washed the sheen of exertion from her face and reapplied a touch of blusher.

When she looked at herself in the mirror, she didn't think she showed any of the desperation rumbling inside her like a different type of hunger.

"Stop worrying," she told her reflection. "You can do this." With a deep, fortifying breath, she retraced her steps to the kitchen, arriving just as a little boy barreled through the back door.

The miniature cowboy skidded to a halt and stared up at her. "Are you Brooke?" he asked as several more people arrived for dinner.

"Yes, I am."

He smiled. "You're pretty."

A few laughs bubbled up from a couple of guys who appeared to be a few years older than her.

"I thought you didn't like girls yet," one of them said, teasing evident in his words to the boy.

"But my nephew is right," the other man said as he looked at Brooke.

She couldn't meet the man's eyes, so she focused on the little boy. "Thank you. You're quite handsome yourself."

He blushed and scuffed his booted toe against the floor. What an adorable kid.

The boy's uncle scooped up the boy. "You gotta wait your turn with the pretty ladies, Evan." The guy tipped his hat and winked at her. "Simon Teague, ma'am."

She managed a smile, though she feared it wavered. "Brooke Vincent. Nice to meet you." Simon topped her by several inches, and he had an air of command and authority about him that had her edging away, hoping he wouldn't notice.

That's when her gaze found Ryan stepping into the room alongside his mom and an older man who must be his father. The elder man was the spitting image of a lifelong cowboy—tanned, lines next to his eyes from squinting into the bright sun, gray hair but still handsome. Like the Marlboro Man when he became a grandfather.

Ryan was just as tall as the rest of the men, but his presence didn't overwhelm her like Simon's had. She couldn't pinpoint why his appearance calmed her blazing nerves, especially when earlier he'd made her all kinds of nervous, but it did. She smiled at him in unconscious gratitude.

Merline Teague clapped her hands to get everyone's attention. "Everyone, I see you've noticed we've got a new face in the kitchen. Brooke has applied to fill the cook's post, and she's giving us a sampling of her culinary skills tonight."

"Looks like she's planning to feed all of Blue Falls," said the man who had teased little Evan about liking girls. By the way he stood close behind the other woman in the room, she'd guess they were a couple and maybe Evan's parents.

"You do know this isn't fair, Mom," Simon said. "You never had Trudy cook on family night."

"Trudy would have told me to go jump in the lake. I figure I have a narrow window of opportunity here."

Everyone laughed, and Brooke felt she was the one person not in on the joke. Did Merline mean she was leaning toward giving her the job and she figured Brooke would soon set limits on her work? She resisted the urge to tell Merline that she'd cook every meal every day if the agony of not knowing could just end.

As the laughter died down, Merline caught Brooke's eye. "Now, let's quit the silliness and let Brooke tell us about what she's made."

Brooke took a breath and dived in. "I've prepared two types of menus—one simple and comforting, the other a bit fancier. You could use the latter for special occasions, like if you were hosting an anniversary party or wedding." She proceeded to tell them about each of the dishes, drawing nods and sounds of appreciation. She hoped they liked everything as much after they tasted it.

"Let's eat. I'm starving." This came from the elder Mr. Teague.

As everyone filed through, filling their plates, Merline stationed herself next to Brooke and introduced her to everyone as they passed by.

"Simon's already introduced himself," she said when the flirty cowboy paused in front of them to nab a piping-hot yeast roll.

"What, you're not going to tell her how wonderful I am?" He smiled as he wrapped his free arm around his mom's shoulders.

Merline looked at Brooke. "This one doesn't have a problem with self-confidence."

"Hmm. I think I've just been insulted," he said.

Merline patted his cheek. "Not at all, dear. Now quit holding up the line."

Simon shot Brooke another smile and winked a blue-gray eye at her before heading for the table.

Next, she met Nathan and Grace, Evan's parents, who were newlyweds despite Evan's age.

"It's nice to meet you," Grace said. "It'll be good to have another woman around here. We're a bit overrun with testosterone."

"And you love it," Nathan said as he bumped the side of her hip with his own, causing Grace to smile up at him.

A pang hit Brooke at how in love these two obviously were. Once upon a time, she'd dreamed of that kind of love for herself.

"And this here is our youngest, Ryan," Merline said as Nathan followed Grace to the dining room and Ryan took their place in front of Brooke.

She had trouble maintaining eye contact with him. Again, she wondered how a man could calm her and make her nervous at the same time.

"We've met," she said.

She noticed the slight widening of Merline's eyes. "You have?"

Ryan glanced from Brooke to his mother. "Yeah. I ran out of drinks, came up here to get one."

Merline shifted her attention to Brooke. There was something seeking in her expression, making it difficult to not squirm. With a slight nod to Brooke, Ryan made his way toward the dining room, as well, to be replaced by his father.

"This is my husband, Hank."

Brooke looked up into the face that was an older

version of his three sons. He extended his hand, which Brooke accepted and shook.

"I'm glad you're here," he said. "Merline has been working too hard lately."

Everyone was acting as if she already had the job. Did they know something she didn't?

Merline waved away her husband's worry and shoved him gently toward the dining room before filling her own plate.

Brooke eyed the people sitting around the table, noticed that two empty seats remained.

"Are you expecting someone else?" she asked Merline.

"No, everyone's here."

"Oh, I could have sworn Ryan said there'd be seven adults."

Merline glanced at the table. "He was counting you too, honey."

A jolt hit Brooke. *Honey.* She could still hear her mother calling her the same thing, and missed it terribly.

The idea that the Teagues expected her to eat with them hadn't even entered her mind. She was the potential help and had planned to nibble on leftovers after they were finished.

"I don't want to intrude on your family night."

"It's not an intrusion if we invite you." Merline caught Brooke's gaze again. "Seems you and Ryan talked about several things."

Something about the way Merline spoke had Brooke's instinct for caution firing. "Just about the number for dinner since I forgot to ask you."

"He should have also made clear that we don't expect you to cook and not eat."

Now that Merline had put the idea of eating in her head, Brooke realized how hungry she was. As if to put an exclamation point on that thought, her stomach growled.

Merline laughed. "Go on and fill a plate."

As Brooke did exactly that, she wondered if the now-retired Trudy had ever eaten with the family. And if not, why was Merline suddenly changing things? Or maybe Trudy had just had a family of her own to get home to, something very much absent from Brooke's life.

When she finished filling her plate, she turned toward the dining room. Awkwardness cut through her like a chilly wind off the Potomac River.

Merline waved her toward a chair between Evan and his uncle Simon. "Come on. Don't be shy."

"Yeah. Shy doesn't work around here," Simon said.

When she took her seat, she looked up and realized Ryan was sitting directly across from her. He averted his eyes, as if she'd caught him watching her.

Or maybe she was just letting paranoia get the better of her, something she'd sworn not to let happen. Whether or not she got this job, she was starting a new life. And she refused to let the old one have control over her anymore.

Despite her determination, however, she still froze when Simon grabbed her hand.

"Oh my God, marry me."

The comment and look of ecstasy on his face hit her as so ridiculous that she laughed—a short burst that escaped before she could stop it.

"What?" Simon asked. "This is the best thing I've tasted in...ever."

"Hey!" Merline said.

"Except your food, of course," he quickly added.

"Well, that's it, I'm afraid," Merline said. "Can't have that kind of competition."

Brooke's heart sank. After all her work, she would leave this ranch as broke as she'd arrived here. More days or weeks living off of her savings.

Simon squeezed her hand and leaned closer. "She's just kidding."

Brooke turned her attention to Merline for confirmation.

Merline grinned with mischief. "I am kidding. How can I not hire you? You've already got at least one of my sons proposing marriage."

Everyone laughed, including Brooke. She used the moment to pull her hand free of Simon's. He seemed like a nice guy, funny, handsome, but she wasn't going down that road again anytime soon. Maybe ever.

"Thank you," she said to Merline.

"You might not be thanking me after a few more days with this bunch."

But as she looked around the table, at the smiling and teasing and obvious love, she couldn't imagine being anywhere else. If she couldn't have that kind of life herself, she could at least bask in the reflected glow of people who did.

When her gaze met Ryan's again, he offered a momentary smile before returning his attention to the food on his plate. Maybe she was crazy, but she had the oddest feeling he'd been staring at her as she was focused in other directions. Her skin warmed at the thought that, as soon as she lowered her gaze, he might do so again.

And part of her really liked the idea that he might want to.

Chapter Two

It took more effort than he was used to expending, but Ryan did his best not to pay undue attention to Brooke. Or to the way his mother kept watching him, as if she knew he was attracted to the new cook. Just last week, Simon and he had lamented their mother's increased interest in matchmaking for her two unattached sons on the heels of Nathan's marriage to Grace.

"She thinks she's one of Cupid's minions," Simon had said as they sat on the corral fence after dinner one night.

"Yeah. She's been bitten by the grandma bug."

"And I don't think Nathan and Grace having another baby on the way is going to be enough to satisfy her. We better keep on our toes and prepare to run fast."

They'd laughed at the time, but now he wondered if Simon had changed his mind. Granted, his oldest brother was the family flirt, but he sure seemed to be trying extra hard this time. That whole impromptu marriage proposal had been a bit over the top, even for Simon.

Ryan tried to ignore the fact that it annoyed him.

Fact was, he should encourage Simon. Brooke seemed nice, could cook like a taste bud's dream come true, and was pretty. No, she was more than pretty.

But he was afraid to put a name to how he thought she looked. He didn't want to risk wanting something he couldn't have. Shouldn't have.

And the last thing any woman needed in her life was him.

"Ryan, why don't you help Brooke with the dishes?" his mom said as they all began scooting away from the table.

"Oh, I'll do it," Grace said.

"Nonsense. You worked hard all day."

Ryan thought about how he'd worked nearly nonstop since daybreak, but he didn't point out that fact, didn't even meet his mom's eyes. Objecting would just draw more attention to the situation and give his mom fuel for her matchmaking fire.

"Sure." He stood and started collecting dishes.

When Brooke joined him in the kitchen, she started loading the dishwasher as he scraped what little was left on the plates into the trash.

"You don't have to do this," she said. "Go on and be with your family."

"I'd rather do this. I think Mom has a Scrabble tournament planned."

"I heard that," Merline called out from the dining room. "Don't think either one of you is getting out of it."

He caught the surprise on Brooke's face that was coated with a layer of fatigue. With a lowered voice, he said, "Don't feel you have to stay."

"No, it's okay. It's good to get to know everyone I'll be interacting with."

Working together, they finished the cleaning by the time his mom got the Scrabble board set up.

"How are we doing teams this time?" Simon asked

as he stepped over Nathan's outstretched legs and took a seat in the living area.

"Guys versus girls," Grace said.

"Oh, no," Nathan said. "You all killed us last time."

Grace smiled wide. "That's why I like that team structure."

"How do you think we should divide?" his mom asked, looking at Brooke.

"Uh...names in a hat?"

"Well, we got plenty of hats," his dad said, grabbing his from the rack by the front door. He tossed it bottom up on the coffee table made from a slab of a huge tree trunk polished to a high shine.

Ryan wasn't sure whether he wanted to be on Brooke's team or not. On the one hand, he had to get used to her and over the initial attraction. He didn't want to deal with the awkward feelings every time he saw her. On the other, what if being around her just increased the attraction? That was a complication he didn't need in his otherwise simple life.

He shook his head, telling himself just to focus on getting through family night. He could do that—he certainly had enough practice.

They ended up on the same team, and in the shifting of positions he found himself sitting next to Brooke on the couch.

She smelled like roses.

He took a slow, deep breath so no one would notice. Of all the flowers, she had to smell like roses. He closed his eyes for a moment, remembering the day when he'd been sleeping on the side of the road outside Baghdad. The air had been choked with dust, heat and sweat, not fit for man or any other living creature to breathe. Out of nowhere, he'd wanted nothing more than to smell roses. It hadn't made sense. The Hill Country was filled with wildflowers, and his family didn't grow roses. But the desire to smell them had taken over and dogged him for days. He'd begun to think the heat had finally used his skull for an oven and baked his brain.

When he'd been shipped back to San Antonio to mend, he'd asked one of the nurses at Brooke Army Medical Center to get him a vase of roses. She hadn't even blinked at his request, making him wonder what other types of odd things broken soldiers asked for after they'd been to hell and back. The scent of those roses had helped him more than the therapy sessions during those early days, convincing him each day that he was truly back home in Texas.

"Yoo-hoo, Earth to Ryan," Simon said.

Ryan opened his eyes, momentarily disoriented.

"It's your turn to draw tiles," Brooke said beside him. Her voice sounded as soft as those yellow rose petals.

He plunged himself fully into the present, drawing letter tiles from the bag and refusing to catch his mother's gaze. He suspected she would be wearing that too-familiar expression of worry for him. She thought she hid it well, but she was wrong.

When he revealed the three tiles to his teammates, Nathan groaned at the *Q*. But Brooke took it and the other tiles and immediately started rearranging letters. He did his best to hide the wide grin that wanted to spread across his face at the word her quick fingers produced. If the other team made the right play, his was going to be off to a great start. Suddenly, a game of family Scrabble didn't seem like such a hardship.

BROOKE KEPT HER expression neutral, but she almost lost it when she glanced at Ryan and saw the edges of his mouth twitching. If she knew him better, she'd be tempted to nudge him in the ribs to keep him from giving away that she had a high-scoring play in the making.

"They've got something good," Grace said as she nodded toward him.

Simon looked up from examining his team's tiles. "What? No one's even made a play yet."

Brooke kept her competitive spirit tamped down until the other team placed their opening word, *stare,* on the board for a total of ten points. Only when she put her team's last tile into its spot did she meet the eyes of her opponents and smile.

The forty points of *oblique* stared up at everyone.

Merline slapped her palms against her knees and laughed. "We've got ourselves a serious player." Her pale blue eyes sparkled, and Brooke recognized the look of excitement at the upcoming challenge.

As play after play was made, Brooke wondered if there had ever been a more raucous game of Scrabble. She found herself laughing along with everyone else, and it felt good, like a massage to her bruised emotions. It'd been a long time since she'd had anything to laugh about. It was nice to be appreciated again, too, and that's exactly how she felt when the various members of the Teague family went back for seconds—or in a couple of cases, thirds—of her desserts.

"I'm going to be fat in a week with your cooking, Brooke," Simon said as he polished off another slice of orange-juice cake.

"You'll just have to find more crooks to chase," Ryan said.

Crooks? She met Ryan's gaze, and he must have seen her unspoken question.

"Simon is our local sheriff. Ranching isn't enough for him. He has to chase bad guys, too." Ryan said it as though it was an old joke, but the revelation caused Brooke's mood to shift. She thought of the last time she'd spoken with police officers and the horrible aftermath. Would Simon be able to tell she was hiding something?

Fatigue settled on her like a heavy, suffocating second skin. As soon as her team pulled out a win, she decided to make her exit. Luckily, it appeared as if everyone else was calling it an evening, too, so she didn't stand out.

"Sorry if it felt like you got a bit of trial by fire tonight," Merline said as she accompanied Brooke into the kitchen.

"It was actually fun. Can't tell you the last time I played a board game."

"Good. Now do you need some time off tomorrow to get settled?"

"No, I can be here whenever you need me." She tried not to think about how early life got started on a ranch and how tired she was.

They nailed down the details of the work schedule for the next few days, and it felt good to have a solid plan instead of the uncertainty that had been her constant companion lately.

"Where are you staying?" Merline asked.

Heat crept up Brooke's neck. "The Rochester." The lofty name did not fit the run-down little motel a few miles outside Blue Falls, but the place had two things going for it. One, the low rental rate. Two, never in a million years would Chris think to look for her there.

"Oh, honey. You can't stay there," Merline said. "It's awful."

"It's okay. I'll look for a more permanent place on my day off."

"No. You can stay here tonight if you don't mind the couch. The bedrooms are full of stuff or torn apart for remodeling. And all the cabins are occupied."

"Really, I'll be fine."

"What about the bunkhouse?" Ryan piped up.

Brooke looked across the kitchen island to where he stood on the other side. He didn't meet her eyes as he twirled an apple that sat atop a pile in a large wooden bowl.

"That's a good idea," Merline said. "It's nothing fancy, but it's clean and way better than the Rochester. Ryan, can you help Brooke get settled in the bunkhouse?"

He hesitated for a moment, as if he might be regretting opening his mouth, before finally nodding. "Sure."

Brooke thought about objecting again, saying she could manage on her own if they'd just point her in the right direction. But she was exhausted, and the quicker she found a bed to collapse on the better. She could go get what little she'd left in her motel room tomorrow.

After another round of good-nights, she followed Ryan outside, smiling at him as he held the kitchen's screen door open for her. Chris had held the door for her countless times, but looking back she realized it was all for show, to keep up his image. With Ryan, she got the impression that courtesy was as natural as breathing, that he would never *not* think to do it. She didn't know how she'd deduced that about him after so short an acquaintance, but she believed in the absolute truth of it.

"The bunkhouse isn't far," he said as they stepped out into the night.

"Good. I think I'm even more tired than I realized."

"You'll sleep like a baby out here then."

She nearly sighed out loud at the wonderful thought. The night before had been anything but restful. On top of her nervousness about her interview was the fact that guests of the Rochester obviously didn't stay there to sleep.

When they reached her used Focus, packed like the proverbial sardine can, she tried not to think how its purchase was another step she'd taken to distance herself from all that had come before. She hated it. Not that there was anything wrong with the car. Goodness knew it was better than the beater she'd driven in high school and college. But it was what it represented. Like staying at the Rochester, the compact blue car was part of a plan to be as little like her true self as possible. The only thing she hated more than the car was Chris—and her own blindness to what he truly was.

"Got any room in there for a passenger?" Ryan asked, a hint of a smile on his face.

She eyed the pile of stuff on the passenger seat. "If you don't mind holding a box. It's that or strap you to the hood."

He laughed. "I'll take the box."

After a bit of rearranging, they got into the car. She knew Ryan was tall, but he seemed even more so wedged into her passenger seat.

"Sorry about the tight fit," she said.

"No problem. We're not going far." He directed her past the barn and down a dirt road that meandered along a fence. It was so dark outside that she couldn't see anything beyond that. She almost commented on it but didn't want her remarks on his home to potentially invite questions about where she was from.

Ryan seemed content to sit quietly. She'd noticed he

was less talkative than his brothers, particularly Simon. She hoped Simon would tire of his flirting if she didn't respond in kind. But she had to be careful not to be seen as rude either. She'd worked with enough hotel convention-goers to be able to deal with lots of personality types, but she'd always known they'd be gone within a week. For as long as she stayed at Vista Hills, she'd have to see Simon.

"There it is." Ryan pointed through the windshield.

Her headlights illuminated a low, rustic building surrounded by sprawling, gnarled trees. Live oaks. While all trees were technically alive, the live oaks seemed more so, as if they had unique personalities. She pulled into a clear area that bore the marks of earlier vehicles.

"Hope you're not expecting four-star accommodations," Ryan said as she cut the engine.

She gave him a raised-eyebrow look and allowed herself to relax a little. "You do remember I was staying at the Rochester, right?"

He smiled. "Good point."

After Ryan got out of the car, it took Brooke a moment to recover from seeing his simple smile up close. It'd been warm, easy, not loaded with expectations.

Maybe Simon wasn't the Teague brother she was going to have to guard against.

"What do you need tonight?" Ryan asked when she got out of the car.

"I'll get it," she said as she started toward the back of the car.

Ryan held up a hand to halt her. "You're in Texas now. Chivalry isn't quite dead here yet."

"You could tell I'm not from Texas?"

"Not enough twang."

This time, she was the one to smile. "I'll have to work on that."

"So?" Ryan nodded toward the car.

She relented and pointed at the backseat. "The suitcase on top."

Ryan retrieved the suitcase then led her toward the bunkhouse. He unlocked the front door and turned on an overhead light to reveal a main room that was half living room, half kitchen like the main house, only on a much smaller, more rustic scale. A nondescript tan couch, two matching chairs and a scuffed coffee table filled the foreground. Beyond the couch was a simple kitchen a few decades out of date with its Formica countertops and a table suitable for a fifties sitcom.

Ryan sat the suitcase next to the couch. "Nobody's lived here in years, not since we started focusing more on the guest ranch than raising horses. All our ranch hands now are married, so they have their own homes."

"It's nice of you all to let me stay here tonight. I'll look for another place as soon as I can."

"No hurry."

Did he want her to stay here at the ranch? She looked away, telling herself she was being silly. Plus, it didn't matter. Ryan Teague was simply her employer's son, would never be more than possibly a casual friend. And it was better that way.

A wave of loneliness as heavy as her fatigue descended on Brooke. Was this the way it was going to be the rest of her life—living a lie and being alone?

"You okay?" Ryan took a few steps closer to her, and she had to fight the deep urge to seek a hug from him, this man she barely knew.

"Yeah, just tired." She hoped he couldn't tell how

choked her voice sounded. She kept her eyes averted so he couldn't see the tears welling in them.

When he didn't respond, she dared a glance and saw recognition in his expression. He knew more than exhaustion was tugging at her, but he didn't push the subject. Instead, he took a step back and gestured toward the two doors on each side of the main room.

"There are four bedrooms with small bathrooms, all pretty much alike. Make yourself at home."

She swallowed against the lump in her throat. This might be where she was starting over, but it wasn't her home. Would any place ever feel like home again?

"I'll go so you can get some rest before you collapse." Brooke started to move toward the door. "I'll drive you back to the house."

He smiled. "I think I can make it."

"You're sure?"

He caught her gaze. "Brooke, go to sleep."

She nodded but still followed him. "Thank you, for everything."

He gripped the edge of the door as he looked back at her, and she found herself focusing on the lean muscles in his tanned forearm. "I didn't do anything."

"Trust me, you did." She wished she could tell him just how much his small kindnesses meant to her, how they'd kept her propped up when she'd been on the verge of collapse.

He seemed to accept her words. "Good night, Brooke."

"Good night."

Despite being more tired than she'd ever been in her life, she slipped out onto the bunkhouse's porch and watched as Ryan made his way down the road, until the night swallowed him.

The moment she could no longer see him, the deepness of the night grew ominous. She told herself it was only the paranoia taunting her again, but she still hurried inside and locked the door behind her. At the end of her ability to think clearly, she stumbled into the first bedroom she came to. She didn't even change before falling onto the bed.

As her eyes closed and sleep started to overtake her, her brain replayed the sight of Ryan walking down the road in the dark. Only this time, he turned just before stepping out of sight and smiled at her. Warmth wrapped her in its embrace, and her heart drifted weightless as a child's balloon. Her lips curved in a return smile as the last light of consciousness went out.

IN THE MORNING, he'd have to find his brain, because he'd obviously lost it sometime since meeting Brooke Vincent. How many times had he told himself to steer away from her since the punch of that first unexpected meeting in the kitchen? So what did he do instead? Suggest she stay at the ranch.

But the idea of her spending another night at the Rochester made his skin crawl. That place wasn't safe, not for a woman with big doe eyes and a vulnerable smile. His fists clenched as he reached the area outside his parents' house.

"Man, what's up?" Simon asked as he descended the front steps. "I go to the john for five seconds and you make off with my girl."

"*Your* girl?" Ryan tried to keep his tone light, but it was damned hard.

"What, is she yours?"

Ryan stopped walking and faced his brother. "She's

not anyone's. Geez, dude, she just got here. You letting Mom's matchmaking get to you?"

"This has nothing to do with Mom and everything to do with that gorgeous new cook. You did notice her being pretty, right?"

Ryan started walking again. "I'm not blind."

Simon stopped at the back of his truck. "Are you interested in her?"

Yes, you fool.

"You know me, would rather be on my own." Ryan met Simon's gaze, well-practiced at not showing what he was really feeling.

And what was that? Anger? Frustration? Jealousy? How could he be jealous when he'd known Brooke less than a day? Maybe it was anger that he no longer considered himself fit for a romantic relationship, nothing more than a casual date, anyway.

Simon seemed to accept his assertion at face value. "So, think she'd go out with me?"

"Not if she's smart."

Simon laughed. "You're no help at all. Man, I wish I had a sister."

And Ryan wished his mom had hired a safe woman, one old enough to be his grandmother.

We don't all get what we wish for, do we?

"Want a ride?" Simon asked.

"What is it with people thinking I can't walk two feet?" Ryan muttered.

"What?"

"No, I'm good." Before he managed to make a complete idiot of himself, he headed toward home.

But when he got there and undressed, sleep remained elusive. Despite a long day in the shop, he stared at the ceiling as awake as he'd been at noon. Might as well get some more work done. He put his clothes back on and trudged out to the shop. He consulted his list of orders but didn't feel inspired to work on any of them.

He sank onto the wooden stool next to his large workbench. He reached for the one thing that got him through nights when sleep refused to pay a call. The block of wood revealed only the hint of an angel's outline. He closed his eyes and mentally scanned the shelf of angels that sat in his bedroom, remembering their details, each one different. When he opened his eyes and ran his fingertips over the surface of the wood, he fixed an image in his mind and started to carve, chipping away to find the angel buried inside the wood.

An hour passed with the chip and scrape of his carving tools against wood the only sound. He lifted the new figure toward his lips and blew away the shavings. An angel stared up at him—an angel with big doe eyes.

Chapter Three

Someone had painted her eyes shut. Or glued the lids together, because they refused to obey her brain's command to lift. Somewhere in her memory lay a reason why she needed to open her eyes, to move, to wake up.

Brooke sat up so quickly the resulting head rush made her blink and press the base of her palm against her temple. Once her vision cleared, pieces of memory switched her unfamiliar surroundings into familiar. She was in Texas, the Vista Hills Guest Ranch, at her new job.

Her job! She looked out the window, at the strong sunlight pouring into the bedroom. She leapt from the bed and raced to her suitcase for clean clothes. No time to shower. As she stripped off the previous day's clothes, she searched the kitchen cabinets for a glass then rinsed her mouth. She paused in putting on a fresh blouse to search her purse for a stick of gum and popped it into her mouth.

Her hairbrush, along with the toothbrush and toothpaste, was back at the Rochester, so she finger-combed her hair as she raced for the door.

Please, don't let me have lost this job before I've even really started.

She yanked the door open then yelped when she

almost crashed into Ryan. Instinct made her lift her hands, and they made contact with his chest in the same moment he grasped her upper arms.

"What's wrong?" he asked.

"I'm late," she said as she tried to catch her breath. She stepped back, breaking the contact between them. "I can't believe I'm late on my first day. I'm never late."

When she skirted Ryan and ran down the steps toward her car, he kept pace with her.

"It's okay," he said. "Mom figured you'd need today to rest and get settled."

"But we made plans last night for me to cook breakfast for the guests this morning."

"She took care of it."

Brooke still didn't pause as she rounded the back of her car. Ryan slipped into the passenger seat as he had the night before. Why was he here?

"You can slow down," he said as she started the car.

"I can't lose this job." She hadn't meant for her desperation to go verbal, but her brain wasn't firing on all cylinders.

"Mom isn't going to fire you."

"You don't know that. Being late on the first day doesn't look good."

"I do know because she's the one who sent me out here to leave you a note saying it was fine if you wanted to start tomorrow." He held up a folded piece of paper.

So he hadn't appeared on her doorstep on his own.

Good. If he wasn't interested in her, that would make interacting with him way easier than with Simon, who'd kept up a constant barrage of flirting the night before. Of course, neither brother was her chief concern at the moment. She raced down the dirt road, leaving a whirl of dust in her car's wake.

"You might want to—" Ryan didn't get the rest of his sentence out before she hit a pothole so hard her teeth slammed together.

"Sorry," she said as she spared a glance for Ryan.

"That's okay. I like whiplash."

Horrified, she slowed to a near stop. "Did I hurt you?"

"Here's a tip. We tend to joke a good amount, so you'll want to learn to tell when we're teasing."

"So, you're okay?"

He leaned against the door. "Yes."

Brooke returned her attention to the road then drove the rest of the way to the main house and parked. She didn't even look at Ryan as she bolted from the car, simply tossing a "'Bye" over her shoulder. If he responded, she didn't stick around to hear.

When she hurried into the kitchen, she found Merline putting away dishes.

"Good morning," Merline said in a cheery voice. "Did you sleep well?"

"Yes, thank you. I'm so sorry I overslept. It'll never happen again." She stepped forward to take over putting the dishes in the cabinets.

Merline placed her hand atop Brooke's. "It's okay. Didn't you get the note I sent?"

"Ryan told me about it, but you and I made arrangements last night, ones I've already failed to fulfill." Her mother had taught her at a young age the importance of fulfilling one's responsibilities, so by being late she felt as if she were failing not only Merline but her mother as well.

Merline squeezed Brooke's hand. "Listen to me. Everything is fine. Your job is secure unless you suddenly poison all the guests. That would certainly be bad for business. I saw how exhausted you were last night and should have told you then to take today off."

"Really, I'm ready to work."

Merline smiled. "Of that I have no doubt." With a final squeeze, Merline returned to her task. "If it'll make you feel better, you can make lunch for the guests. They'll be back from a wildflower tour then."

"Thank you."

They worked side by side the rest of the morning, preparing lunch for the twenty guests. Brooke's heart twinged because the situation reminded her so much of days spent in the kitchen with her mother. The two women looked nothing alike. Merline had a silver bob and remarkably smooth skin for a woman her age. Brooke's mom had looked more like an older version of Susan Sarandon, but with a tougher life. Despite the differences, Merline's kindness started to fill the hole left by Brooke's mom's death.

"You seem to lose yourself when you're cooking," Merline said as Brooke slid two cherry pies from the oven.

"I'm sorry. Did I miss something?" She could hear her mother's voice, commenting on Brooke's constant daydreaming. Back then, she couldn't wait to leave home, see something new, be someone important. Now, she'd give anything to be able to step into her mother's West Virginia kitchen and feel her comforting arms around her.

"No. I was just watching the look you get when you're cooking, like you're in another world."

Brooke sat the pies on the island to cool. "There is something about it that takes me away."

"That's how I feel when I'm painting."

"You're an artist?"

"Evidently." Merline laughed. "It's a recent realization. We're beginning to be overrun with creative types around here. I'm painting. Grace does interior design. Ryan's furniture."

Brooke nearly looked up at Ryan's name but caught herself in time. She'd picked up on just how much Merline had talked about her sons throughout the morning, particularly the two unmarried ones. She wondered if Nathan's recent wedding had Merline on the hunt for wives for Simon and Ryan. Brooke swallowed, wondering if she'd ever be able to trust a man enough again to be willing to get married. After all, she'd thought Chris was going to be that man.

How wrong she'd been.

If there was anything in her life to be grateful for, it was the fact that Chris had shown his true colors, the man he was behind the mask of his public persona, before she'd had the misfortune of marrying him.

Thankfully, the guests returned, and talk of available Teague sons was replaced with feeding hungry tourists. As she served food and made small talk, she relaxed even more. It felt a little like her old job, making convention guests happy. Only now she accomplished the task by preparing chicken salad and cherry pie rather than consulting with chefs on the fare for special events and hotel guests on the perfect meeting space.

She insisted on doing all the cleanup while Merline retreated to her home office to work. Once Brooke was finished and had planned for dinner, she spread out the local classifieds on the dining room table.

She skipped over the sections that held no interest before locating the For Rent listings. With red pen ready to circle possibilities, she started reading. As it turned out, she didn't need the pen. What few availabilities she found came with pricey rental rates attached, no doubt a result of Blue Falls being a popular tourist destination.

Brooke closed the paper, already planning to seek information about neighboring communities. How far would she have to go to find something more within her budget? She feared she'd encounter the same problem throughout the Hill Country.

"Find anything?" Merline pointed at the newspaper as she walked into the dining room.

"Not yet. But I'll get a room in town until I do." And try not to cringe at the price of the temporary space to lay her head at night.

"Don't be silly. I was thinking, why don't you live permanently in the bunkhouse? It's just sitting out there. You could fix it up however you like."

The convenience beckoned Brooke. Plus, she liked the idea of not having to venture forth from the ranch more than necessary. She had to believe that the longer she was gone, the less Chris would look for her. Eventually, he'd stop. At least that's what she told herself.

"Only if I pay rent."

"I think we can work something out. Now, I'm running into town for a while. Do we need anything?"

Brooke shook her head. "I'm going to do some meal planning this afternoon and may shop after that."

"Sounds good. See you at dinner."

Brooke decided to use the sliver of free time she had to go check out of the Rochester. But when she walked outside, she noticed the right rear tire on her car was flat.

She sighed, imagining a day when everything would go perfectly—none of this one step forward, two steps back stuff. She straightened and took a deep breath. No focusing on the negative. She had a job and a place to stay. Compared to only a few short weeks ago, today was absolutely peachy.

Telling herself that things could be so much worse, she opened the trunk and started pulling out boxes and bags filled with pieces of her life. Winter clothes, books, childhood mementoes. By the time she reached the spare tire, sweat was rolling down her back and stinging her eyes.

"Come on, damn you," she said as she tugged the tire out of the trunk. When it finally came free, she stumbled and nearly fell on her butt. The tire slipped from her slick fingers and landed with a thunk. She eyed the tire then mashed it with her foot. Also flat.

"You've got to be kidding me." She kicked the useless ring of rubber.

"Careful. It might kick back."

Brooke wiped the sweat from her eyes so she could see who was speaking. Nathan stood a few feet away.

"Sorry I didn't see you sooner or I would have come out to help," he said.

"It's okay."

"Looks like you're in need of some tire patching."

"That or I just shoot the car and put it out of its misery."

Nathan smiled. "Perhaps a bit drastic. We've got a friend with a garage in town. He can fix the tires in no time. Dad and I can't get away right now. Have to give some riding lessons. But Ryan can probably run you into town."

"I don't want to inconvenience anyone."

"He won't mind." Nathan pointed down the driveway. "Hang a left at that mailbox. Ryan's place is back there."

So he lived on the property, too. She'd wondered

since he tended to pop up often, but she hadn't wanted to cause speculation by asking.

"Okay, thanks."

Nathan tapped the front edge of his hat. "Glad to help."

After Nathan returned to the barn, she shoved her belongings back in the trunk before heading for Ryan's.

No matter how much she told herself she couldn't be interested in Ryan Teague, part of her wasn't having it. In fact, denying the attraction seemed only to make it stronger. Her nervousness grew with each step down the driveway. When she reached Ryan's mailbox, she stopped and stared up the hill in front of her. Somewhere beyond that hill was a good-looking man who did funny things to her pulse without even trying.

She shook her extremities like a runner trying to rid herself of tension before a race. Maybe the key to getting past this initial attraction was to just acknowledge it—but only to herself. Okay, so Ryan was totally drool-worthy, and he seemed like a nice guy. Based on appearances alone, he was the kind of guy dreams were made of.

But dreams sometimes turned into nightmares.

Stop it!

Brooke took in a slow, cedar-scented breath. No more thinking about the past. From this moment on, she was Miss Looking Forward, at whatever the future might bring. As she started up the hill, her steps fell lighter against the gravel. Hey, she liked this new positive attitude. She felt as if she was shedding anxiety on the road behind her. It could stay there and be ground down even further on her way out. Maybe she'd give it a swift kick for good measure.

At the top of the hill, she spotted Ryan's home—

a small cabin with what looked like an outdoor wood-shop at one end. She wondered what kind of furniture he made. Curiosity as much as necessity drove her forward.

She scanned the outside work area as she approached. Tools and wood shavings lay scattered across a tall workbench. Freshly cut pine and a hint of past fires filled the air. She stepped into the shade provided by the shop's roof. That's when she heard cursing from inside the house. She edged closer to the open door.

"Ryan?"

He jerked at the sound of her voice, turning enough that she was able to see the blood on the hand he held under a stream of water flowing from the kitchen faucet.

She rushed toward him. "Oh, Ryan, what did you do?"

"Knife slipped." His words came out slowly, and now that she was closer she could see how pale he looked.

Brooke took hold of his arm and gently guided his hand back under the water. He closed his eyes and shook as his blood began to mix with the water flowing down the drain. She had to distract him so he wouldn't pass out.

"Where are your clean hand towels?"

After a moment's hesitation, he opened his eyes a fraction. "Drawer in front of you."

She retrieved a mostly white towel and set it on the counter next to the sink. "So, how'd you manage this feat of brilliance?"

"Unparalleled talent?"

She laughed. If he could joke, maybe he wouldn't collapse in the middle of the floor. "I've heard of putting blood, sweat and tears into your work, but this seems a tad excessive."

When she squeezed some soap into her hand and proceeded to wash the wound on his left palm, she noticed he gripped the edge of the sink tighter with his other hand.

"We're almost done." She rinsed the soap away then shut off the water. Careful not to hurt him more than necessary, she pressed the towel against the wound and lifted his hand level with his shoulders. With her other hand pressed against his back, she guided him toward a comfy-looking chair facing his TV.

"I'm fine," he said just as he reached for the back of the chair to steady himself.

"Yes, I can see that."

"That sounded sarcastic."

"Really?" She smiled when he looked at her. "I had no idea. Now, how about you sit before you fall?"

He didn't argue. Once he was seated and holding the towel against his cut, she returned to the kitchen and grabbed a glass from the dish drainer. As she filled it with water, she tried to get her racing pulse under control. She was here just to help him, not to think about the texture of his work-roughened hands or the hard heat of his back. Not how pretty his eyes were up close. Not how easy she found it to be with him, especially in the past few minutes when parts of her true personality had shown themselves.

Get a grip.

She took the glass of cold water back to Ryan. "Here." She extended the glass as she sat on the end of the coffee table in front of him. When he reached for the glass, she resumed pressing the towel against his palm. "I think you need a few stitches."

Ryan shook his head. "It'll be okay."

"This part of one of those tough-guy routines?"

"No. Just don't like hospitals."

"You and most of the rest of the population."

"Really, no need for stitches. I've had worse."

Something about the way he said it, low and far away like the previous wounds were as much emotional as physical, kept her from insisting he go to the hospital. After all, she couldn't force him.

"Okay, then, where are your first-aid supplies?"

He met her eyes and she got the feeling that he changed whatever he'd been about to say. "Under the bathroom sink."

As she walked farther into his house, she couldn't help the feeling that she was also stepping deeper into his life.

Ryan's bathroom was classic bachelor. Single towel hanging over the shower rod. Shaving cream, razor, hairbrush and a half-used bar of soap on the sink. No frills. Even with so little to see, it felt strangely intimate to be standing in the midst of it. Her gaze drifted toward the shower and her imagination started forming a picture of Ryan below an entirely different flow of water. She jerked her attention back to the sink and knelt to retrieve the first aid supplies.

When she stood, Brooke eyed her reflection in the mirror. She hadn't even thought before running into Ryan's house to help him. Not that she could have left him alone and injured, but it had felt oddly natural. Maybe they were just in the early stages of an easy friendship. That certainly would be nice. New life, new friends. As long as she didn't get too close.

"You find everything?" Ryan called out.

"Yeah." She returned to the living room.

"I've stopped bleeding like a stuck pig," he said.

"Yay, progress." Brooke resumed her spot on the end of the coffee table. "Looks like your color's coming back, too. You were pulling a Casper a few minutes ago."

"Can't say I'm a fan of the sight of blood." There it was again, an echo of meaning beyond the actual words.

She took his hand in hers, ignoring the zing of unwise awareness, and removed the bloodstained towel. "Then I suggest not stabbing yourself."

When he smiled, she smiled back. "I'll keep that in mind," he said.

She cleaned the wound, washing away the last remnants of blood, then applied antibacterial cream and a gauze bandage.

"She cooks, she plays a mean game of Scrabble and makes a pretty fair nurse."

"A necessity when your sister is the clumsiest person on the planet." Brooke wasn't sure why she'd said that, but Holly's various mishaps had been what sprang into her mind. She hadn't revealed too much, and if she kept too private that might invite as many unwanted questions as being too open. The trick was finding the right balance between saying enough but not too much.

Mentioning Holly brought on a wave of homesickness—not for her condo in Arlington but for the mountains of West Virginia and her older sister, her only remaining family.

"You all right?" Ryan asked.

"Yeah." Brooke realized she was still holding Ryan's hand so she released it and scooted back on the table. "How does your hand feel?"

"Like some idiot stabbed it with a carving knife."

"Hey, accidents happen."

He glanced out the door toward his shop. "But never at a good time."

"Is there ever a good time to stab yourself?"

He lifted his good hand from the arm of the chair then let it drop. "You have a point."

"Is there anything I can help you with?"

"You a wood carver by chance?"

"Nope, sorry." She stood and walked toward the door. "Anything else on your to-do list?"

"I have a table and chairs ready to deliver. Maybe I can get Simon or Nathan to help."

"Or me." She lifted her hands, holding the palms out, and wiggled her fingers. "See, two good hands."

"You looking for a second job?"

"How much you paying?"

He raised an eyebrow. "How much do you charge?"

She crossed her arms, hugging herself against a flicker of innuendo she thought she might be imagining. She leaned against the doorframe. "Actually, I just need a ride into town. You might be the idiot who stabbed himself, but I'm the idiot who barreled into that pothole this morning."

"And you have a flat."

"Two."

"Talk about going overboard."

Laughter bubbled up in Brooke. "What can I say? I'm an overachiever."

Ryan rose from the chair, steady on his feet this time. In the small space, he appeared taller, broader. Had she just made an offer that would have her spending more time with him instead of less? Had she spent too much time in the sun while digging out that useless spare tire?

Or had the feel of Ryan's hand in her own caused her attraction to overrule her common sense?

Of the two idiots in the room, she was definitely the bigger.

Chapter Four

Ryan decided not to examine his reasons for accepting Brooke's offer too closely. He was just going to stick with the fact that he needed help until his hand healed. He still couldn't believe the klutzy move. It was a wonder the U.S. Army had ever allowed him to pack a gun.

"Turn here." He pointed to the street coming up on the right. "We'll drop off your tires first so Greg can have them ready before we head back to the ranch."

Brooke made the turn. She'd grown quiet on the ride into town, but it didn't bother him. For the most part, he wasn't a chatty guy. He'd already talked to her more in their short acquaintance than he had to some of his neighbors in months.

"Hey, there's your mom." She pointed out his side of the windshield.

"Yeah, that's her art gallery."

"She has a gallery? Wow. She mentioned painting, but I had no idea it was a profession."

"It's still pretty new. Grace runs her interior design business out of there, too. Also has the new-car smell."

Brooke smiled. "You Teagues seem to be a talented bunch." She nodded toward the furniture riding in the bed of the truck. "Including you."

"It's a living."

"It's art as much as painting."

He barely knew this woman, but that simple praise from her sent a wave of warmth through him.

"I can't imagine doing anything remotely artistic," she said.

"But you do. With food."

She glanced at him. "That's different."

"Why?"

"It's just a job."

"Building furniture is just my job." Granted, he enjoyed it, but wasn't that what you wanted from a job, something that wasn't drudgery? "Do you not like cooking?" He'd have sworn otherwise.

"Oh, I love to cook. Just never thought of it as art before. At least not what I prepare."

"Take it from the guy whose fanciest dish is mac and cheese from a box, what you do is art."

She smiled. "Maybe I should autograph all my dishes then."

His own smile responded to hers. "Maybe you should."

He directed her to Greg's garage then hopped out to find his friend. Greg wandered out in his grease-stained jeans and Longhorns T-shirt, wiping his hands on a shop towel.

"Hey, Ry. What's up, man?" That's when Greg noticed Brooke approaching. "Damn, I heard the new cook was hot, but Simon was holding out."

Ryan suspected Brooke was close enough to overhear. "Classy," he said and punched Greg in the shoulder. "I told her you could fix a couple of flat tires this afternoon. Don't make me into a liar."

Greg extended his hand. "Greg Bozeman, ma'am. And for you, all these other jokers can wait."

Ryan noticed a touch of unease in Brooke's eyes as she shook Greg's hand, and he got the feeling it didn't have anything to do with Greg's grease-stained fingers. Maybe she just didn't want to encourage any flirting. Goodness knew she was getting enough of that from Simon.

"Thank you," she said. "I appreciate it."

"How are you liking your new job?" Greg shoved his hands into his pockets, as if trying to hide them. Brooke seemed to have all the men she met acting out of character.

"I like it."

"I see you're having to beat these Teague boys off with a stick." He gestured toward Ryan's bandaged hand.

Brooke looked startled for a moment then recovered. "No, he managed that all by himself."

"No doubt to earn some sympathy from a pretty lady."

Ryan resisted slugging Greg again. "On that note..." He turned for the truck. "Get those tires done or I'm going to Bernie's next time."

Greg laughed. "I'll believe that when I see it."

After Greg retrieved the flat tires, Brooke climbed into the driver's seat. Ryan thought about offering to drive, but truth was his hand was throbbing as though he'd stabbed a spear right through it."

"So Bernie's is the competition?" she asked once they were back on the road.

Ryan barked out a laugh. "If you can call him that. He's eight hundred if he's a day, and he piddles with cars on the days when he doesn't decide to run a roadside taco stand or go into the Christmas-tree farm business."

"The resident jack-of-all-trades, huh?"

"And master of none."

Brooke drove slowly through the main part of town. "Blue Falls seems like a nice place, slow-paced."

She sounded as if part of her liked the idea of the laid-back way of things here and part didn't know quite how to adjust to it. He resisted the uncharacteristic urge to delve into her past. It wasn't his business, and he never said anything that invited others to ask about his past.

"It's home."

Before they headed to the Rochester, they made the side trip to the Mayfairs' house to deliver the table and chairs.

"Looks like you've got an eager customer waiting." Brooke indicated Rob Mayfair standing on the edge of his front porch.

"Yeah, we're trying to get this inside before his wife, Julie, comes home. It's an anniversary gift."

"That's very sweet." Brooke parked close to the porch and cut the engine.

As soon as they exited the truck, Rob shot them a wide smile. "You must be doing well, son, if you've got a chaffeur now."

Ryan held up his bandaged hand. "Needed some extra hands."

"Well, I'm sure hers are a damn sight prettier than yours."

"Definitely." Ryan glanced at Brooke in time to notice a flush to her cheeks. He wasn't prepared for how that simple, innocent look punched him in the chest.

How could one simple, offhand word from a man she barely knew make her cheeks warm? No, it had to be the heat. She just wasn't used to this crazy Texas oven-roasting. D.C. got plenty hot and humid in the summer, but this Texas heat was a different breed. You could bake a loaf of bread out here.

She shook Mr. Mayfair's hand as Ryan introduced them and was glad when they cut the chitchat and started moving the table and chairs inside. They became the centerpiece of a small dining room decorated in a warm, country style. She looked closer at the new furniture and saw how Ryan had incorporated little details like tiny carved apples around the edge of the table and on the backs of the chairs. Apples that looked remarkably like the ones on the room's wallpaper border.

She couldn't imagine Chris ever noticing that kind of detail, making that type of connection with any of his clients. But that wasn't what they paid him for, was it? Brooke shook away the image and the chill it brought. Chris was the last thing on which she wanted to expend any mental energy. Too much of her life had already been lost to him.

"You've outdone yourself," Mr. Mayfair said as he stood back and admired Ryan's craftsmanship. He pulled a checkbook out of his back pocket.

Ryan quoted a figure that surprised Brooke, not because it was high but rather amazingly low.

"That's not the price we agreed on," Mr. Mayfair said.

"I took a little longer than I projected, and I'm having a sale this month."

Ryan and Mr. Mayfair stared at each other for a long moment before the older man nodded. Brooke thought she saw a glimmer of tears in his eyes, but he bent to write the check before she could be sure. He handed it to Ryan and shook his uninjured hand.

Then Mr. Mayfair turned his attention to her. "Try

to make sure this one doesn't hurt his other hand. No matter how talented he is, I don't think he can carve with his toes."

She smiled at that image and Mr. Mayfair's easy friendliness."I'll try." She didn't know what else to say. Despite her offer to help Ryan, she wasn't going to be spending all her time with him. But she couldn't really explain that without it looking odd either.

Once they were back in the truck and headed toward the Rochester, she glanced at Ryan. Despite her pledge to herself to keep a bit of distance, she had to ask one question.

"You aren't really having a sale this month, are you?"

"For him, I am," Ryan said, answering as if he'd been expecting the question. "Julie just went through a battle with cancer, and he wanted to get her something really nice. He told me she'd seen some of my furniture in a shop in town and really liked it. But he's been working two jobs just to pay the medical bills."

Brooke's heart swelled at the story and at Ryan's act of kindness. "That was really nice, what you did."

He shrugged, like he was uncomfortable with the praise, like what he'd done was no big deal. "They need the money more than I do."

A surge of admiration for Ryan had her finding him even more attractive. Before she and Chris had crossed paths, why couldn't she have met a man like Ryan?

Geez. Listen to her. One kind gesture and she was ready to believe he was perfect. But it wasn't a lone act, was it? Her brain ticked off all the kindnesses she'd seen him undertake in their brief acquaintance.

Telling her how many guests to cook for, suggesting she stay in the bunkhouse, calling Greg to get her tires fixed, and now the thoughtfulness toward the Mayfairs.

Still, she knew the interstates through Texas better than she did him. While not every man hid a dark side the way Chris had, that didn't mean she was going to trust the first interesting one to come along. She was willing to go with friendship, but no more.

She popped over a hill, revealing the sad sack of a motel that was the Rochester. At night, it'd been less than appealing with its faux adobe facade and window AC units in various states of disrepair, but in the full daylight it took pitiful to new levels.

Ryan laughed beside her.

"What? It was just a place to sleep. Well, attempt to sleep."

"No, I was remembering this time in high school when Dad caught Simon trying to get a room here with a girl. I think Simon still winces when he thinks about it."

"Bad, huh?"

"Oh, yeah. Dad gave him every horrible chore he could find, and even made up a few. It was like an episode of *Dirty Jobs* on steroids."

Brooke laughed at the image. "I've known your brother less than twenty-fours hours, and somehow that story fits."

"Ironic that he's now the one who has to come out here and roust kids out of this place. Though most of them have gotten wise and go to Austin now."

She stared out the windshield at the motel of way yesteryear. "I can't imagine."

"Sneaking off to a motel with a boy?"

"When I was a teenager? My dad would have had my hide. And I'd have been the lucky one."

"Tough guy?"

She thought about it for a moment. "Just protective."

A trickle of sadness made its way through her. If only someone had protected him.

"You okay?"

She nodded. "I'll just be a minute." When he started to get out of the truck, she paused. "I didn't leave very much here."

He took her words the way she intended, that she didn't need help collecting her belongings. Though he knew this ratty motel better than she did, a well of embarrassment bubbled up at the idea of him seeing inside her room, at what running for her life had reduced her to, though he wouldn't know the reason why.

When she stepped into the drab little room with its icky floral polyester bedspread and cheaptastic furnishings, she couldn't believe she'd actually stayed there, that she'd convinced herself it was okay. She wasn't an elitist, but it wasn't okay that she'd been forced to stay in a dump motel at the crossroads of Nowhere and Edge of the Earth. Who in the world had ever thought this was a good location for a motel? Blue Falls looked like a booming metropolis compared to the dusty stretch populated by the motel and equally run-down gas station.

But the moment she stepped out of this room, she was closing the door on more than bad carpeting and scratchy towels. She was also locking away a chapter of her life she'd like to delete as easily as she could a computer file. To say she was tired of running, of making every decision as if her life depended on it, would be the Goliath of understatements. And she was done.

She tossed her few personal items in the overnight bag and headed back out into the strong sunshine. Its heat burned away the lingering feel of dismalness the room imparted, and she took a deep breath. She felt good. The shock of that realization nearly made her stumble as she headed toward the office to check out. All her careful planning had brought her a second chance at life, and she was determined to enjoy it. No more timid mouse. That *so* wasn't her personality, and she'd been angry at Chris all over again every time she found herself looking over her shoulder or refusing to interact with people more than absolutely necessary.

Could she do it? Be her old self, the one untainted by the gradual erosion perpetrated by Chris so expertly she'd not realized it until it was too late? She ventured a quick glance at Ryan sitting in his truck. Though she told herself it was a good thing he wasn't watching her, that unfortunate nugget of herself that still wanted to mean something to someone shrank in disappointment.

With a shake of her head, she strode toward the motel office and found the same gray-haired, chain-smoking woman who'd checked her in. Brooke placed her key—the shove-it-in-the-lock kind, no key cards for the Rochester—on the scuffed countertop.

"Leaving us already?"

As fast as I can. "Yes."

"I see you're with Ryan Teague." The woman lifted her eyebrow, asking for more details without saying the words.

"Yes, I'm working at the ranch. Had a bit of car trouble this morning, so Mr. Teague was nice enough to bring me by to pick up my things."

"You're staying with the Teagues?" The woman sounded as if she couldn't wait to get on the phone and spread the word the moment Brooke left, as though she was the president of the local chapter of Gossips of Texas.

"I have my own place." This woman didn't need to

know it was at the ranch. Brooke didn't offer any further information and kept her face blank, so the woman was left with being uncomfortably nosy or simply taking Brooke's key and money. After a few suspended moments, the woman chose the latter.

Brooke accepted her receipt and headed for the door.

"Enjoy your new position," the woman said.

Despite what she thought might be some innuendo, Brooke mumbled a "Thanks" without looking back. It bothered her that this woman, who shouldn't even matter, was making her feel dirty and possibly assuming things about Ryan that weren't true. When she reached the truck, she slid into the driver's seat without meeting Ryan's eyes.

"Let me guess," he said. "Jo Baker was working?"

"I don't know her name."

Ryan leaned forward and looked past her toward the office. "Yep, that's Jo. Old crow."

That unexpected assessment surprised Brooke enough that she met Ryan's eyes. For a moment, they ensnared her. They were so pretty, and she'd bet all the money she had that he had no clue what kind of effect they could have on a woman.

"Well, she is," he said, evidently responding to the look of surprise she must be wearing. "I've never met anyone nosier in my life." He nodded out the windshield. "That's why she runs this place, so she can pass along who is sleeping with whom."

Brooke shook her head as she started the truck's engine. "That's sad."

"Did she say something to upset you?"

Brooke looked over her shoulder and backed out of the parking space. "No, I'm fine."

She didn't meet his eyes as she turned back around,

not wanting to see any more questions there. She didn't want him to detect how Jo's simple words had made her feel small and unable to take care of herself. It reminded her too much of what some of her former coworkers must think of her. Of how embarrassed she'd been when she'd last seen her sister and sworn her to secrecy.

Ryan fell silent until they rolled into Blue Falls. "You hungry?"

"I've got to get back to the ranch, prep for dinner."

He nodded and redirected his attention out the side window. He shifted in his seat, as if sitting on the passenger side felt awkward. She opened her mouth to initiate some conversation but found herself at a loss. The urge to ask him about himself nearly found voice, but she had to remember that she didn't want to reciprocate. Maybe someday, but not now. Until she was sure she was safe, that anyone near her would be safe, she had to keep a barrier around herself. She might let some of her natural personality find its way to the surface in the coming days, but that was all.

By the time they reached the garage, Brooke was nearly twitching in her seat as well. And she wasn't sure why. All she knew was that she breathed a momentary sigh of freedom when they reached the garage and she hopped out almost before the engine stopped turning.

"Ah, the pretty lady returns," Greg said when she stepped into the first bay of the garage.

She couldn't help smiling at him. Greg was a charmer, and her instincts were telling her he was harmless. And despite how those same instincts had failed her before, she believed them this time.

"My tires ready?"

"Good as new." He grabbed one of the tires and made

short work of carrying it to Ryan's truck as Ryan strode toward the bay to retrieve the second.

When she started to object, he said, "I still have one good hand."

There was no difference in the action taken by Greg and Ryan, but something about the strength and fluidity of motion she saw as Ryan slung the second tire into the truck bed made her heart beat a little faster.

As he started to turn back toward her, she averted her eyes a moment before he would have caught her staring. Instead, her gaze met Greg's, and she spotted realization there. In that split second, she made the decision to pretend he hadn't seen anything. Because he hadn't. There was nothing there to see. And if she told herself that enough, maybe it would eventually be true.

"Thank you for fixing the tires so quickly."

"You're most welcome." The combination of drawl in Greg's voice and his slight nod made it easy to imagine him as some chivalrous movie cowboy from the John Wayne era. Sort of like everything she'd seen from Ryan. The similarity actually helped her confused feelings. Maybe there wasn't anything special about Ryan after all. Maybe they just grew them chivalrous in Texas.

She reached into her purse for the money to pay Greg.

"No need for that," he said. When she started to object, he held up a hand. "Call it a welcome-to-town deal."

"Don't let him fool you," Ryan said as he leaned against the front of his truck. "He's just angling for a free meal at some point."

Greg made a show of being hurt by the suggestion, the expression so absurd that in the next moment the three of them were laughing. Like three friends. A lessening of the weight pressing down on Brooke made her imagine a real future in Blue Falls, one filled with friends, laughter and a sense of belonging. One where she didn't always have to look over her shoulder or wonder if Chris stood around every corner. It couldn't happen soon enough.

Chapter Five

"Thanks for the help today," Ryan said as Brooke parked his truck back beside his home.

"You're welcome." She gestured toward his hand. "You do know there are easier ways of getting help than skewering yourself, right?"

A small grin pulled at his mouth. "I'll remember that for next time."

"Also remember to keep it cleaned and put a new bandage on it each day."

"Yes, ma'am."

She let her hands slide from the steering wheel into her lap. "Sorry. I sounded bossy, didn't I?" She didn't like to think of herself as bossy, but for so long she'd been a take-charge kind of person. It had gotten her out of West Virginia, through college and into a nice career. Too bad it hadn't kept her from being a blind fool.

"Nah. I've heard worse," Ryan said, drawing her back to the here and now.

After a moment of quiet invaded the truck's cab, Brooke grasped the door handle, needing to put some space between her and Ryan. "Well, I'd better get back to work. See you at dinner?" Now why had she asked that?

"Probably not tonight. Got a lot of work to do, and I'm going to be slower than usual."

She nearly asked if she could help, but she cut off the words' means of escape. Tomorrow was soon enough to offer a helping hand again. She didn't want to seem overanxious to spend time with him. If she had any sense, she wouldn't be.

"Okay. If you don't mind, I'll come back for the tires after I'm finished with dinner tonight."

"Go ahead and drive the truck up to your car. I won't need it for a day or two. Dad can help you change the tires since I'm currently pretty useless in that department." With that, he slid out of the truck and shut the door behind him. He waved then headed inside without looking back.

She ignored the traitorous part of herself that wanted him to turn around and gift her with one more glance at his face.

With a sigh of frustration, she started the engine and headed back to the main house, where she planned to bury her unwise attraction in preparing pulled barbecue pork and sourdough bread.

When she hurried in the back door of the Teagues' house into the kitchen, she found Merline putting the finishing touches on a meringue pie.

"You didn't have to make dessert," Brooke said. "I'm sorry if I was gone too long."

Merline licked a bit of meringue off her finger. "Honey, we're going to have to cure you of this constant apologizing. You're an employee here, not a prisoner."

"Oh, I didn't mean that. It's just…"

"You were helping Ryan."

"Uh, yes."

"That doesn't happen often, him accepting help. He's usually the one doing the helping."

Brooke considered whether she should tell Merline the reason why but decided it was best to disabuse her of any potential matchmaking notions. "He hurt his hand this afternoon and needed help with a delivery."

Merline froze and gripped the edge of the island. "He's hurt?"

Something about the inordinate amount of fear on Merline's face made Brooke want to ease it. "Just a cut, nothing serious. He was carving and a knife slipped."

A slow breath escaped Merline. "You're sure?"

"Yeah. I just dropped him off. He was going back to work."

Merline smiled, but it looked forced. "I guess a mother never stops worrying about her babies."

Instinct told Brooke there was more going on here, but it wasn't any of her business. "So, what kind of pie did you make?"

Merline smiled again, more genuinely this time, and spun the pie around a little. "Lemon meringue."

"That's my favorite. I'm sure the guests will love it."

"Now you go ahead and make whatever you'd planned. Don't mind me. I just like to bake sometimes."

For some reason, the unspoken words "as a stress reliever" popped into existence in Brooke's head. She walked closer to Merline and leaned against the island.

"Are you okay?" Now that she looked closer, Merline appeared tired.

Merline waved away her concern. "Yes, fine. Just trying to adjust to juggling a few extra balls in the air."

"The gallery? Ryan told me it's pretty new."

"Yes. It's a great lot of fun, but it's also more work

than I expected. Although Grace pitches in when she's not too busy with her own work."

"Maybe you could get some help. I bet one of the colleges has an art or business student who'd jump at the opportunity to get some experience, maybe some internship credit."

"Now there's an idea I hadn't thought of. My dear, you might be a genius at more than cooking."

Pride and appreciation warmed Brooke. It seemed like forever since she'd felt good about something she'd done, something that wasn't undertaken in the name of self-preservation.

Feeling closer to Merline than their short acquaintance could account for, Brooke playfully shooed the older woman out of the kitchen. "Go on, investigate getting an extra pair of hands and let me be a kitchen genius."

Merline laughed as she headed for her small home office, and Brooke found herself standing in the impressive kitchen wearing the biggest smile she had in weeks. Months.

Brooke spent the rest of the afternoon easing into her new post a little more, letting herself enjoy the simple pleasure of kneading dough and mixing ingredients, of inhaling the aromas of fresh-baked bread and carrot cake. She even giggled a little as she used her finger to scoop out and eat the remainder of the cream cheese frosting. Man, it felt good to relax.

As the ranch guests started filing into the dining room for dinner, she placed the various dishes on the sideboard buffet style, telling the hungry guests about each one.

"You're going to have to roll me out of here in a

wheelbarrel," one middle-aged man said as he patted his belly, making his teenage daughter roll her eyes.

"It is a ranch," Brooke said. "I'm sure they have one around here somewhere."

"That we do, and we know how to use them," Merline said from where she stood visiting with the guests at the next table.

Laughter rang out around the room. That and the compliments she received throughout the meal added to her improving mood. Still, by the time the guests had finished eating and Brooke had cleaned up the dishes and put away the leftovers, her long day was catching up with her. It wasn't late, but she was ready to go to bed nonetheless.

"You're good with the guests," Merline said as she walked into the kitchen after locking up the dining room for the night.

Brooke put the last of the non-dishwasher-safe pans away. "It's an interesting group. Did you know Mr. Brinton runs a hot-air balloon company in Albuquerque? I've always wanted to try that."

"Oh, you should. There's nothing quite like it. We actually met the Brintons when we went to the Balloon Fiesta out there a couple of years ago."

The idea of soaring above everything seemed so incredibly peaceful, sailing away from the world and all its troubles. She'd have to do that someday, when she felt secure again.

"Any luck finding some help with the gallery?"

"As a matter of fact, yes. A wonderful young student at UT, who just happens to be studying art and business."

"Well, that seems meant to be."

"It does, doesn't it?"

The tone of Merline's voice, like she was talking about more than an intern, caused Brooke to pause and catch her gaze. But all Merline did was smile.

"Well, I'm going to pack it in. I think the trip here is still catching up with me."

"Yes, you go get some rest. I'll see you bright and early in the morning."

Why did Brooke think Merline sounded a little too bright herself? Chipper, even.

Well, why shouldn't she be? She had a great family, a wonderful home, two successful businesses. There had been a time when Brooke had thought she'd had it all, but had she ever radiated sunshine the way Merline Teague did? She didn't think she liked the answer.

With a final good-night, Brooke headed out the door. It was then that she remembered the two flat tires. She considered retracing her steps, seeing if Mr. Teague could help her change them, but she was too tired to deal with it. She'd cajole one of the ranch hands with his favorite dessert in the morning.

As she rounded the edge of the house, she noticed someone in the glow of headlights next to her car. Someone in boots, jeans and a cowboy hat. And her car was sporting a newly inflated tire, giving the dumpy little thing a full set of four.

Her heart rate picked up despite her inner voice telling it to calm down. She'd missed seeing Ryan at dinner, even though he did mighty inconvenient things to her brain and nerves. With a deep breath, she headed toward him. "You shouldn't be doing this." She'd feel horrible if he injured his hand further because of her.

As she drew closer, he turned around and tipped up the front of his hat.

"Since when has it been a crime to help a pretty damsel in distress?"

Not Ryan. Simon.

She nearly skidded in her effort to stop her forward progress. "Simon."

"In the flesh."

The word "flesh" made her uncomfortable, even though Simon had done nothing to make her think he was anything other than another of the crop of chivalrous cowboy types that were thick in these parts. She wasn't fond of the "damsel in distress" moniker either. She'd had quite enough of that label, was determined never to wear it again.

She took a couple of steps back under the guise of eyeing her newly fixed tire. "You didn't have to do this."

"Were you going to do it?" He leaned casually against the back of her car, not crowding her.

"Well, no."

"So I am the hero of the hour."

Brooke couldn't help laughing a little at his grand pronouncement. "This usually works, doesn't it?"

"What?"

She made a waving motion that encompassed the tire and him. "The flirting."

He smiled wide. "Yes." He shifted and crossed his arms. "But it's not working with you. I must be losing my touch."

"I'm just not the best target for your efforts."

"Got your eye on someone else?"

"No."

"You sure about that?"

She schooled her features before looking up at him. "Let's just say I'm taking a break from guys and leave it at that."

He eyed her for an uncomfortably long moment. "I'm never one to argue with a lady."

"A wise policy."

He barked out a laugh at that. "Would you like help unpacking all this?"

"No, but thank you." Just the idea of unpacking tonight made her a hundred times more tired.

"Okay. I'll take Ryan's truck back."

Brooke caught herself just before she asked him not to. "Thanks."

She slid into the driver's seat of her car and tried to mentally erase the idea that she'd looked forward to having the truck as an excuse to see Ryan again. What was she thinking? Ryan might be the world's nicest guy, but right now she needed time to focus on herself, to get back to a place where she trusted her judgment. She didn't need to be thinking about how disappointed she'd been to find Simon next to her car instead of his younger brother.

RYAN NEARLY INJURED himself again when he heard the sound of his truck's engine coming up the drive. With a curse at his sudden clumsiness, he tossed aside the chisel to land in a nest of wood shavings. Why had she come back tonight when he was covered in sweat and sawdust?

It shouldn't matter.

But it did.

Some part of his brain was screaming that he'd neglected his desires too long, that here was a woman who had awakened something inside of him that he'd cold-cocked to keep it asleep. No matter how many times he'd told himself since meeting Brooke that he wasn't ready for feeling anything yet, his damned emotions had flipped him the bird and done what they wanted. He was attracted to Brooke Vincent, intensely attracted, and that was that.

He wondered if he had the willpower to keep from acting on that attraction. He barely knew the woman, but gut instinct told him she deserved more than he could give. That edge of vulnerability she tried to hide told him that loud and clear.

He made a token effort at wiping his hands and the sweat off his forehead before stepping out of the indoor portion of the shop that jutted off the side of his house. His mood fell into his boots when he saw Simon walking toward him with his truck keys instead of Brooke.

No, this was better, the dose of cold water in the face he evidently needed to remind him that he was damaged goods and had a valid reason for keeping to himself.

"Heard you went galivanting all over the county with Brooke today."

"I'd hardly call delivering a table and getting busted tires fixed galivanting."

"And the Rochester."

"I see Jo is still the biggest mouth in Texas."

"Actually, it was Pete, who was pretty surprised to see your truck there."

"I hope your deputy has better things to do than gossip about whose truck is where."

"Touchy tonight, aren't you?"

Ryan lifted his bandaged hand. "You would be too if you nearly shoved a knife through your hand. Throbs like hell."

Ryan regretted bringing up his injury. Concern on his mother's face, he could deal with. His big brother's was a bit much to swallow. He wasn't a snotty-nosed little brother tagging along after Simon and Nathan anymore. He'd been to war, for God's sake.

And come out the other side not quite himself.

"Then I'd suggest not doing that again."

Ryan snorted. "How do you stand yourself, being so smart?"

"It's tough."

Ryan shook his head. "Have you eaten? I can slap some PBJ together."

"Nah, I grabbed a burger on the way back from serving a warrant out in the hinterlands."

"The glory of being sheriff."

"Some days I think you've got it right, a job where people aren't pestering you 24/7."

"You, a hermit? Not in this lifetime. You love all that attention."

"I could do with a little less of the mischief makers and a lot more female attention."

"Is there any available woman left in this county you haven't dated?"

"A few. The lovely Miss Brooke for one."

Ryan clenched his fists for a moment before forcing himself to relax. He hoped the limited light hid his reaction. "You asked her out yet?"

"No." Simon sighed. "Didn't get the chance before she made it known she wasn't interested."

"Ow, bet that smarts."

"I think her interests lie elsewhere."

Ryan did not meet his brother's eyes, did not ask his meaning. "Or maybe she's been in town five seconds and doesn't know anyone yet." And a really annoying part of himself was glad for that fact. Seeing Greg's and Simon's interest in Brooke made him realize he had to squash his attraction to her or do something about it.

"No, don't think that's it." Simon wore his I'm-the-older-brother-and-thus-know-more expression. It'd been annoying when Ryan was a kid and hadn't gotten any less so with age.

"Sure you don't want something to eat? I'm starving."

"I bet you are." No missing the meaning behind the words.

Ryan faced Simon then. "Don't push this."

"Come on, man. I know it's hard, but you've got to start living again sometime."

"I live every day. I'm not in that damned hospital anymore. I can even walk without a noticeable limp now. Haven't had any freakouts in a while. What else do you want from me?"

"That's *existing*. I want you to *live*."

They so rarely spoke to each other without some layer of teasing involved that the pure, honest look on Simon's face unnerved Ryan, made him twitchy. And though he'd never be able to admit it out loud, it touched him deeper than he'd ever imagined possible.

Simon didn't wait for an answer. Instead, he tossed the truck keys to Ryan. "Go on in and eat. Your stomach rumbling is going to wake up half of Blue Falls. Don't need them calling the station thinking we're having an earthquake."

When Simon was halfway back to the ranch's main driveway, Ryan wandered inside but didn't make the PB or J. Despite the persistent growling of his stomach, he didn't know if he could eat. Too many questions swirled through his head, ones he'd been blessedly free of two short days ago. Before Brooke Vincent had strolled into his mother's kitchen and into too many of his thoughts. It was as if she'd flicked on a switch the moment she'd popped her head out of that refrigerator and he'd met her eyes for the first time.

He leaned his palms against the edge of the kitchen counter, pressed his eyes closed and cursed. Damn it, Simon was right. Ryan hadn't truly realized he wasn't living until she'd sent a jolt through him, like a freaking defibrilator starting his heart again.

His stomach growled so loudly this time that he wouldn't have been surprised if the guests in the cabins heard it. He retrieved the ingredients and slammed together a sandwich, ate a quarter of it in one bite. When the sandwich didn't calm his stomach or the hurricane in his head, he ripped open a bag of corn chips and started eating those.

Could he do it? Could he be like Simon and just go out for a casual date? He tossed the bag of chips onto the counter without bothering to close it with one of the clothespins he kept on hand for that purpose. When had he ever been like Simon? He wasn't the love-'em-and-leave-'em type.

That wasn't fair. He'd never heard any of Simon's dates complain afterward. They knew what they were getting.

But Brooke wouldn't know what she was getting if Ryan dared to ask her out. She wouldn't know he came with the kind of baggage it was damn near impossible to unload, no matter how hard you tried.

The kind of baggage he didn't deserve to unload on anyone else because it was his and his alone to bear.

BROOKE STRETCHED, LOVING the feel of having enjoyed the best night of sleep she'd had in months. She might be living in a ranch bunkhouse, but she doubted she could have slept any better at the four-star hotel where she'd worked not so long ago. She couldn't help but feel as though she'd taken a giant step just by sleeping soundly and without nightmares.

In fact, her dreams had been far from scary scenes of being chased and attacked, of having to submit. Her body flushed at the memory of what she'd been doing in that dream world right before she'd woken to the first birds chirping in a new day.

Her, Ryan, a bed the size of Texas and little else.

She flung the covers aside, the embarrassment hot on her cheeks—and other places.

If she'd had any doubt before, it was gone now. She'd lost her mind somewhere between Virginia and Texas. If she backtracked, would she find it dusty and neglected on the side of the road?

As she brushed her teeth and eyed herself in the bathroom mirror, she thought about how different things would be if Chris had never asked her to dance that first time, or if she'd said no. She wouldn't be having these interior battles about her attraction to Ryan. She likely never would have met him.

Thinking a shower might help clear her head, she turned on the hot water and hopped in. But the feel of the water on her skin only served to remind her of the sensations she'd ridden in her sleep.

She toweled off, wiped away part of the fog on the mirror and stared at herself again. "You sure can get yourself in a mess, can't you?"

But this time, she would remain in control. She was here to work, to rebuild her life, not fall for another good-looking guy.

No, Ryan wasn't good-looking, not in the same polished, designer suit way Chris was. He was rough around the edges, a touch mysterious, private, all the things Chris wasn't. Was that why she was attracted, her survival instinct pointing her toward the opposite end of the spectrum?

No. The voice came out of nowhere to speak in her mind, clear and true. So clear that she looked around to make sure she was alone before realizing it was her own voice.

Great. Not only had she lost her mind, she was also talking to herself.

With a good shake of her head, she headed out of the bathroom and got dressed for another day. Despite her chatty brain, she felt good and decided to focus on that. She felt so good, in fact, that she was going to fix her mom's French toast for breakfast.

As she walked along the roadway leading from the bunkhouse, she breathed deeply of the fresh air, drawing even more strength from it. Instead of the hum of traffic, she heard the scurrying of creatures in the trees and the lovely songs of birds she couldn't identify. It reminded her of the simple pleasures of her childhood, before she'd decided she wanted more than her small hometown could give her. But she'd gotten more than she'd bargained for.

A flash of color made her stop and stand perfectly still. After a few moments, the most brilliantly colored bird flew from one branch to another, giving her a clear view of its bright orange belly, green feathers and blue head.

"Hey there, pretty," she said.

The bird chirped in response, making Brooke smile. Her mom must be smiling down on her this morning. First the idea to make the French toast, and now a beautiful bird. Her mom had loved watching the birds in the backyard of their West Virginia home. She'd kept a birding guide and a pair of binoculars in the window over the kitchen sink, always ready to pause in her work to appreciate her "chirpers."

As she approached the back door to the main house, she started to use the key until she noticed Merline and Hank sitting at the island, drinking coffee and reading the paper.

"And here I thought I was going to be the first one in here this morning," she said as she stepped inside.

Merline lifted her cup. "Have to get up pretty early to beat us to the coffee."

"Old habits die hard," Hank offered. "There's fresh coffee, though you don't look like you need it this morning."

"I haven't slept that well in ages."

Merline picked up the coffeepot and refilled her cup. "Glad to hear you're settling in nicely."

"Can I fix you all anything?"

"We'll just have whatever the guests are having."

"French toast, it is."

Hank made an appreciative sound.

Merline laughed as she slid a section of the paper toward her husband. "You've just made a friend for life."

Brooke smiled and pulled a carton of eggs from the refrigerator. "Well, if you like French toast, you're going to love this. It was my mom's recipe, and I've never tasted anything better."

This morning, it didn't hurt to talk about her mother, and she couldn't pinpoint the reason why. Maybe seeing the bird, maybe finally feeling as though she could take a deep breath and let it out slowly. Whatever the reason, she was thankful for it, and she let the memories of Saturday mornings eating breakfast in her princess gowns in front of television cartoons wash over her.

Before the guests arrived, she slid two servings of the French toast in front of Merline and Hank. The moment Hank took a bite he closed his eyes and chewed slowly, seeming to savor every bite. When he swallowed, he opened his eyes and looked at his wife.

"Whatever we're paying her, it isn't enough."

Brooke smiled widely as she prepared enough French toast to feed the twelve guests on the schedule for this morning. As she headed to the dining room, she replayed Hank and Merline's compliments on their breakfast. She was happy to be sharing her mom's recipe with people she was pretty sure her mom would have liked. It helped make her feel like her mom was still with her instead of gone these past four years.

"I hear the world's best French toast is being served here this morning," Ryan said when she finally returned to the kitchen after talking with the guests about where they were from, what they did and their plans for the day.

"You heard right." She crossed the tiled floor to the stove, noticing the elder Teagues had vacated the room. "But you're cutting it mighty close." She scooped a generous helping of toast onto a plate and handed it to him along with a small pitcher of warm syrup. She tried not to hold her breath, waiting to see if he liked it. Instead, she turned and started putting glasses and utensils in the dishwasher.

"You gotten any more marriage proposals since you been here?"

Her attention jerked back to him. "What?"

He held up a forkful of toast, dripping with syrup. "Because this is awesome."

His praise warmed her more than any other. "I'm glad you like it."

"So, that offer to help me still stand?"

"Sure," she said, trying not to appear too eager. "Another delivery?"

"No. Just got some work that requires one more hand than I currently have at the ready."

An image of what his two hands had done to her in that early morning dream threatened to burn her clothes right off her. "Okay." She turned away, taking a deep, silent breath.

"I've got to run into town first, but I'll be back in half an hour or so," he said.

She nodded without looking at him. "I'll be done here by then."

By the time he'd finished his breakfast, she was a nervous wreck wondering if he was watching her. She'd have to use the time he was gone into Blue Falls to pull herself together and recapture the calm she'd felt on her walk to work, remind herself that having the crazy hots for her boss's son wasn't the best idea she'd ever had.

She nearly jumped when he placed his plate in the sink.

"Thanks again for breakfast." He was so close, she'd swear his breath caressed her cheek. Her inhale brought in his manly scent of the outdoors and honest work. Chris had never smelled like that, even after a workout, but she found herself thinking Ryan smelled like honesty. And that was headier than any cologne.

"You're welcome."

Brooke fought the crazy urge to turn slightly, to see just how close he was, what he might do. Before she had time to act on that thought, he was out the back door.

She closed her eyes, gripped the edge of the sink and exhaled. Then, unable to resist, she walked into the family dining room and watched as he headed back toward his slice of the ranch, doing more for a worn pair of jeans than any high-dollar model could ever dream of doing.

She was in trouble, and she wasn't sure she minded it.

Chapter Six

The little girl made Ryan nervous. He kept envisioning her cutting herself like he had, and her father, a prospective customer, not being terribly happy about it.

"Sweetie, don't touch that," the man, an attorney from Dallas, said to his little girl as she reached for the wooden leg destined for a dining room chair. "As I was saying, I'd like to have a desk and chair made for Haylee, something her size."

Ryan didn't know why the man would spend that kind of money on custom furniture the little girl was going to outgrow in short order, but maybe he had plenty of cash to toss in various directions.

"I can do that. Any particular style?" Movement out of the corner of Ryan's eye drew his attention. Haylee was reaching for a handsaw. But before he could intervene, Brooke stepped into the shop, between Haylee and those dangerous, jagged edges. He sent her a silent, thankful expression and returned to his conversation with Mr. Briggs. He counted it as a miracle that he was able to concentrate on what the man said when his attention kept straying to Brooke. She was keeping Haylee occupied by using a thin piece of cast-off wood to draw pictures in the coating of sawdust on the floor.

Several details and a down payment later, he breathed

a sigh of relief when Haylee left the shop unscatched with her father, totally oblivious that her daddy had just forked over a substantial sum on her behalf.

He glanced at Brooke, who was examining his work in progress. "You have great timing."

"She was a curious little thing, wasn't she?"

"I was having horrible visions of emergency rooms every time she reached for something."

"Speaking of injuries, how is your hand today?" she asked as she gestured toward his bandaged hand.

It felt like it was going to fall off, but he wasn't going to tell her that. "Fine."

She crossed her arms and cocked an eyebrow. Something about her was more…alive, more real today. She didn't seem as guarded, and he wondered why.

"Now why don't I believe that?" With a shake of her head, she walked toward him and grasped his hand. "Good grief, this bandage looks like you've clawed your way over a rocky mountain. Don't you wear gloves when you're working?"

It took him a moment to adjust to the feel of her holding his hand, to remember he was supposed to answer her. "I don't like to. They just get in the way."

With another shake of her pretty head, she tugged him toward the house. "Let's at least clean it up and put on a new bandage then."

If it had been his mother trying to take care of him, he would have shaken her off. Wouldn't want her coddling. But he liked the feel of having Brooke near him, showing concern for him, touching his hand. Wise or not, he was going to indulge, at least for a few minutes. Didn't he deserve at least that much?

Instead of depositing him in the main living area, she guided him all the way to the bathroom then started pulling supplies from the cabinet over the sink. With quick efficiency, she cut off his ratty bandage and pointed toward the sink.

"Wash it really well with hot water and soap."

He had to smile at her commanding tone, so at odds with how she'd acted that first night when she'd been trying to land her job. She looked up and caught him smiling.

"What?"

"You're pretty when you're bossing someone around." Had he just said that out loud? Was he flirting? Damn, he was glad Simon wasn't here. His big brother would have a field day with this.

Her cheeks pinkened as she lowered her gaze to the countertop and opened the bottle of hydrogen peroxide. Damn if that extra color in her cheeks didn't make her even more beautiful.

He turned on the hot water and squirted soap into the palm of his injured hand. "Sorry if I embarrassed you."

She shrugged. "It's okay. Guess I have take-charge tendencies no matter how much I try not to."

"Why would you try not to?"

She opened her mouth but froze before words could come out. He got the oddest sensation that she was scrambling for what to say. He knew he should say something to let her know she didn't have to answer, but he didn't. Truth was, he wanted to know more about her. And he knew that wasn't fair in light of the fact that he didn't want to reciprocate and spill any beans about his past.

"Let's just say I'm starting over, new life and all."

She looked uncomfortable, and he'd swear he could feel the tension coming off of her in tangible waves. He searched for some way to ease her.

"Sometimes that's good." His attempt at putting her at ease was weak, but it was all he could offer without opening up and letting his own fresh-start story spill out in all its gory detail.

She simply nodded and handed him a towel to dry his hands. After he did so, she took his hand in hers again. He nearly moaned at the soft, feminine touch. How could something so simple affect him so deeply? He'd touched other women's hands while shaking hands or during the occasional dance at the music hall, but he'd never wanted to have any of them lift her palm to his face, to run her fingers over his entire body, leaving sparks in their wake.

After using a cotton ball and the peroxide to clean his wound even more, she examined the injury more closely by turning his hand this way and that. "Despite the ill treatment, I think you're beginning to heal."

"My job requires working with my hands."

"Most do." She folded a piece of gauze several times. "I'm going to pack it heavier over the wound to cushion it more while you're working."

He watched, mesmerized, as she rebandaged his hand, taking care to cause him as little discomfort as possible. Not once did she meet his eyes. He probably shouldn't have said what he had about her being pretty, but it was the God's honest truth and had seemed a crime not to tell her so.

When she was finished, he examined her handiwork. "You're good at this. If you ever get tired of cooking, you could have a future as a nurse."

"Ugh, no thanks. I've bandaged my share of cuts and scrapes and burns, but I can't handle much beyond that."

"Sounds like your sister must have been really accident-prone."

"A tomboy, at least when we were young. Wouldn't know it now. She's settled into being a regular Miss Domesticity."

"White picket fence, huh?"

"Barbed wire, actually. Her husband's a dairy farmer."

He didn't think she was aware of the quiet sigh and the look of longing tugging at her features.

"You don't get to see her often?"

She hestitated before answering. "Not as often as I'd like."

Ryan feared he'd asked too much as she turned and walked out of the bathroom. After silently cursing himself, he followed.

"So, what's on the agenda this morning?" she asked. "I can help for a little while but need to get back in time to fix lunch."

"It shouldn't take long. I just need you to hold a piece while I finish carving a design. It's too big to put in the vise, and my hand's still too blasted sore to hold it in place."

He led the way back into the indoor part of his shop and pointed to the bottom end of a headboard.

Brooke ran her fingers over the wildflowers he'd already carved along the edge of the headboard. "This is beautiful."

Her praise lit a light inside him. "It's for the Wildflower Inn by the lake. They're adding a couple of new rooms, and I'm doing the furniture for them."

Her fingertip traced the outline of one of the bluebonnets. "Appropriate."

"Yeah, this is wildflower country. Can't throw a stick without hitting some business with 'wildflower' in its name. Sometimes I think they should have named the town Wildflower."

She smiled. "I like Blue Falls. It's very evocative."

He liked how she talked sometimes, with an easy sophistication that wasn't showy. Like it was something she'd cultivated to add to who she'd always been, not replace it.

With a mental shake, he pointed at a spot on the wood. "Can you press down there? Stand up against the edge, too, so it doesn't slip. This shouldn't take long."

He picked up one of the smaller gouges and set to work, forcing himself to focus on creating shapes in the wood rather than the sound of Brooke's soft breathing or her trim legs pressed against the bottom edge of the headboard. He would not think about how a headboard went on a bed, and a bed had a thick mattress, and what you could do with a beautiful woman on said mattress. He clenched his teeth and gave himself a mental slap.

"How long have you been making furniture?"

"Just a couple of years."

"Really?" She sounded so surprised that he looked up.

"Yeah. Saw a magazine about woodworking and thought I'd give it a try." That magazine had been one of, God, hundreds he'd gone through during his hospital stay. He would have read the tax code if someone had given it to him, anything to keep his mind off what had landed him in that hospital bed.

His hand shook just enough that the gouge slipped out of its intended groove, but he caught it before he made like a fool and injured himself again. He knew better than to think about that day so far away when he was working.

"You okay?"

Brooke didn't miss anything.

"Yeah, just a tough spot in the wood." And he hated lying to her. It felt profoundly wrong.

"What all do you make?" she asked.

"Tables, chairs, beds, chests of drawers, armoires, desks, you name it."

"I can see the allure," she said with a dreamy quality to it. "It seems like a peaceful way to spend your days."

She had him pegged without even knowing it. After his tour of duty, he couldn't imagine being around people all the time. Some were fine, he wasn't totally antisocial. But the idea of working in an office all day made him twitch. So he'd served out the remainder of his service time in a hospital bed then come home.

"Is that how you feel in the kitchen?"

"I guess. It's quiet time to think. But I like talking to the guests, too, learning where they're from, what they do."

"Who knows, maybe somebody you know will stroll in one day. People come from all over."

When she didn't respond, he looked up to see she'd gone still and some of the color in her face had drained away. "Brooke?"

"Yeah?"

"Are you okay?"

"Yes, fine. I think it's just taking me a while to get used to the heat here."

He believed that about as much as he believed everyone in Texas would suddenly give up their trucks for compact cars and stop eating barbecue. But he didn't press her, even though the sudden change bothered him.

After a few more minutes of carving, he finished the necessary gouge and chisel work on the headboard. "There, that's done."

Brooke stepped away and wandered across his shop as he smoothed the edges around the carved designs. She lifted a birdhouse from the shelf and looked at it from every angle. "This looks like your parents' house."

"It is. Mom's birthday is coming up in a couple of weeks, so I made that for her."

"It's beautiful." She slid it carefully back into its spot on the shelf. "There certainly are some pretty birds around here. I woke up listening to them. I saw one this morning that was so colorful, he would have been at home in a rainforest."

"Blue head, orange and green feathers?"

"Yes."

"That's a painted bunting, one of the males."

"Interesting how the male birds are always so much more striking than the females. My mom loved cardinals, and lots of people don't realize the bright red ones are the males. The females are brown."

He noticed she referred to her mom in the past tense. More curiosity tugged at him, but he kept quiet.

"Do you need help with anything else?" she asked as she turned toward him.

Yes. He needed help in figuring out how to not be so attracted to her, to not want to know every little detail about who she was. To not want to take her face in his hands and kiss her.

He mentally shook away that image. "No, I can handle everything else. Appreciate the help."

She smiled for a moment. "Then I'll be getting back to work. You should take a break and come up to the house for lunch."

"I doubt the guests would appreciate sitting next to me in the middle of a workday."

She took a few steps toward the door and glanced at

him for a quick moment. "They won't be sitting in the kitchen."

He knew as soon as she said it that come noon, he'd be sitting at the island willing to eat whatever she had on the menu.

BROOKE EXPERIENCED THE oddest urge to skip on her way back to work. It had felt as though she was swimming beyond the safe zone when she'd invited Ryan to come eat lunch in the kitchen, but she'd chosen to ignore the warning alarms bleating in her head and go with it. And something about the look on his face, something indefinable, told her he'd be there. Was there a possibility that Simon wasn't the only brother who wouldn't mind spending time with her? After all, Ryan had told her she was pretty.

It had been so unexpected that she'd bolted like a rabbit at the sound of hunting dogs. But her entire body had filled with a delicious warmth that soothed the bruised and battered emotions she'd shoved into the dark places inside her.

But now that she had the space to look back on it without him right next to her, that solitary sentence spoken in his sexy voice made her smile wide. A part of her whispered that Chris had been flattering and charming in those early days, too, but she shushed it. Just because she was basking in a compliment didn't mean she was going to get serious with Ryan. Considering his family was her employer that wasn't a good idea anyway. But still, after everything she'd been through in the past year, it felt so incredibly good to have something positive to focus on.

By the time she reached the kitchen, she couldn't wait to start cooking. Her feet felt light as she made Amish-style potato salad, mint chocolate cookies and mouthwatering chicken salad on sourdough, the recipe for which she'd coaxed out of the chef at the Davenport. She was just setting out the crisp lettuce, slices of tomato and pickles when the back door opened and in walked Ryan.

Though he still wore his work clothes, she didn't think she'd ever seen anything sexier than worn jeans and a faded green T-shirt accessorized by a cowboy hat and boots that had seen their share of use. Now she fully understood the attraction to the cowboy mystique. There was something primal and deep-seated that reacted to it, yearned to be closer to it. She reined in those thoughts the way the Teague brothers had no doubt reined in countless horses.

"Looks like I'm just in time."

"My mom always said the one thing a man would never be late for was a meal."

He laughed a little and hung his hat on the wall rack next to the door. "My stomach's been grumbling for half an hour just thinking about lunch."

She liked to think of herself as independent, even when she'd been going through all the trouble with Chris, but it gave her a powerful sense of satisfaction to serve lunch to this man. He worked hard, really worked, with his hands, and he was kind and giving.

Stop right there, the voice inside her screamed. *You're in danger of losing yourself to a man again.*

I didn't lose myself to Chris. He took over when I didn't expect it.

Brooke turned away under the guise of setting the rest of the food into the dining room for the guests. She needed a few moments to shove memories of Chris away, to remind herself that being friendly with Ryan was okay as long as she remembered to not go too far.

The guests filtered in, chatting about everything they'd seen on the wildflower tour they'd just returned from and showing each other photos on their digital cameras. After a little chitchat, Brooke returned to the kitchen to find Ryan had cleaned his plate and was nabbing another cookie.

She laughed. "You *were* hungry."

He held up one of the mint-chocolate cookies. "Don't let Simon have any of these or he'll be down on one knee with a diamond ring and booking the reception hall."

Brooke rolled her eyes. "I would venture your brother is the biggest flirt in all of the Hill Country."

"You'd win money on that bet."

"Does it usually work for him?"

"Amazingly well, which has always been annoying."

Brooke laughed again as she felt herself slip a touch more into the Teagues' lives.

Merline entered the room through the back door. "Everyone sounds like they're having a good time in here."

"Ryan was just telling me about Simon's well-honed skill of flirting and how no woman in the Hill Country is safe."

Merline shook her head. "That boy will be the death of me one of these days. Everyone else I know, it's their youngest who is the wild one. Me, it's the oldest. Guess I should just count myself lucky he didn't rub off too much on the younger two. I love him, but I don't think I could have handled three of him."

"Well, that makes Nathan and me sound boring," Ryan said.

"Not at all. I didn't say you two were angels, now, did I?"

Brooke smiled at the mock affront on Ryan's face.

Merline walked over to the sink and washed her hands. "Please tell me there's food left. I'm so hungry I was about to gnaw off my arm."

"There's plenty. Let me fix you a plate."

While Brooke filled her boss's plate, Merline wandered into the guest dining room. After a round of hellos, she said, "I've got a wonderful surprise for you all. A friend of mine runs a tour boat on the lake here, and he wants to try out some dinner cruises this summer. So we've set it up to where you all get to be the first guests. Now, I know you've been spoiled by Brooke's delicious food, but rest assured Lon's wife, Amelia, is a wonderful cook as well."

Brooke listened through the open double doors into the dining area as the guests asked questions, and Merline filled in the details.

"I guess I'm cooking for a smaller crowd tonight," Brooke said, actually looking forward to a little break. Maybe she could even get her car unloaded.

"Honey, you don't have to cook at all," Merline said as she returned to the kitchen. "You're going on the cruise, too. We all are."

Brooke half expected Ryan to object, but he didn't. She couldn't help hoping, just a little, that maybe it was because of her.

Chapter Seven

Brooke nearly locked herself in the bunkhouse and stayed there. In fact, for a few minutes she did when the reality of what she was doing and how she was thinking hit her like a bag of bricks. Nothing had happened between Ryan and her, and yet everything felt as if it was moving too fast. She'd never needed a rebound guy after any other breakup, so why was she leaning toward one now?

Maybe because none of those other breakups had left her feeling alone in the world, ripped from even her true identity.

She sank down on the edge of her bed, braced her elbows against her legs, and pressed the base of her palms against her forehead. The thing was, Ryan Teague didn't feel like a rebound guy. She'd swear something more was going on inside her, and maybe even on his end. But how could she be sure he wasn't just someone who'd hurt her again?

She couldn't. And that uncertainty was even scarier than thinking what she was feeling toward Ryan wasn't just the need to attach herself to someone so she wasn't alone.

Why was she waging a war inside her head? It wasn't as though they were going on a date. There was going to be a boatload of people enjoying the lake cruise. And, honestly, it sounded really nice to have a night of leisure. Pulling herself together, yet again, Brooke surged to her feet and started going through the two bigger suitcases she'd just lugged inside the bunkhouse.

Right now, Ryan had the makings of a friend, and goodness knew she needed one of those just about more than anything. If she focused on that instead of her unwise attraction to him, maybe she'd stop making herself crazy.

Remembering her resolve proved difficult, however, as she rode beside Ryan into town in the backseat of his parents' truck. He wore clean jeans, a newer-looking pair of boots, and a crisply pressed chocolate-colored shirt. And he smelled heavenly, all fresh, simple soap with a hint of pine. She wondered if her willpower to not lean over and sniff his neck would run out before they reached the boat launch.

What didn't make matters any easier was when she caught Merline watching her in the rearview mirror, the older woman had a smile on her face that made Brooke feel as if she was on an episode of *Texas Matchmaker.*

That was it. No matter how late they got back tonight, she was clearing out her car and driving herself from now on.

"Here we are," Merline said as they pulled into a parking area next to the lake.

Finally.

Brooke mentally congratulated herself for not leaping from the truck and her awesomely powerful attraction to Ryan. Once her feet hit the ground, she didn't even have to extricate herself from her riding companions. Little Evan did that for her.

"Hey, Brooke!" He broke away from his parents and ran toward her.

She leaned down to look him in the eye. "Hey, yourself." She tapped the front of his cowboy hat, a miniature version of his father's. "You're looking mighty handsome tonight."

She couldn't tell for sure, but she thought his cheeks turned pink at her words. That made her smile even wider.

"So, you want to be my date tonight?" she asked.

"You're not with Uncle Ryan?"

Brooke froze and refused to look at Ryan, whom she could sense was standing close by.

"Evan," Grace scolded, a horrified edge to her voice. She stepped up behind her son as Brooke stood. "I'm sorry about that. I don't know where he gets these ideas."

"Mom, I got it from—"

"Shush."

From his mom? Grandmother? Why in the world would the entire Teague clan be trying to set Ryan and her up? They barely knew her, couldn't possibly know if she was a good match for him.

Grace gave Brooke an awkward grin. "Glad you could join us tonight, Brooke. I hear this excursion is really pretty."

Brooke eyed the western sky, deciding to pretend the matchmaking undertones weren't obvious. "It's going to be a lovely sunset."

Grace seemed relieved by the change in subject. During her few interactions with Grace, Brooke had sensed a kindred spirit and wondered why.

Brooke held out her hand toward Evan. "Shall we?"

After a quick glance toward his uncle, Evan lifted his

hand and took Brooke's. Together they headed toward the gangplank onto a small version of a paddlewheeler with *Lady Fleur* painted in flowing script down the side. She'd swear Evan grew a couple of inches beside her he stood so tall. She pressed her lips together to keep from smiling at his effort.

When they reached the boat, a tall, white-haired man she assumed was Lon extended his hand. "Welcome to the *Lady Fleur*," he said.

She retrieved her hand from Evan and shook hands. "Thank you." After stepping to the side, she looked down at Evan. "And thank you for helping me on board."

"You're welcome," he said, even trying to sound more like a man than a boy of six years.

She caught Grace's gaze again, but this time there was laughter in her expression as Nathan scooped up his son, causing a riot of giggles.

"I'm guessing he watches every move his dad and uncles make, doesn't he?" Brooke asked Grace.

"Like a hawk. I have to constantly remind them to be careful what they say. They're still getting used to having a kid around the ranch."

In the bustle of guests coming on board, Brooke and Grace separated themselves from the rest of the Teague contingent and strolled toward the bow. Though she wanted to glance back, to feast her eyes on Ryan again, Brooke resisted. No need to feed the fires of speculation.

"So you haven't lived at the ranch long?" Brooke ventured when she felt the need to fill the silence between them.

"Just a couple of months." She looked back toward where Nathan likely stood. "Nathan and I just found each other again after several years apart. Guess you could call it a second-chance-at-love thing."

"That's romantic." Despite everything, her romantic-at-heart nature miraculously hadn't been extinguished.

"Yeah," Grace said with the dreaminess of a woman deeply in love.

Brooke tried to guard against the pang of loss and loneliness but wasn't too successful.

"You like Ryan, don't you?" Grace asked out of the blue.

Brooke stopped in her tracks and was helpless to keep her mouth from dropping open.

"Don't worry, I'm not here to push you or to share that little tidbit with Mama Matchmaker."

"So I wasn't imagining that?"

"Merline?" Grace laughed. "No. It seems one of her new missions in life is to marry off the other two boys and fill the ranch with hordes of grandchildren."

"I knew I should have taken that job at McDonald's."

Grace laughed as she stopped at the railing and looked out across the lake. "Don't let it bother you. She might be eager, but she won't go too far. She's a big believer in people being with their true love."

"I'm not even sure there is such a thing." Brooke hadn't known she even felt that way until the words came spilling out. When she considered how happy Grace and Nathan looked together, she backpedaled. "For me, at least."

"Maybe. Maybe not." Grace drummed her fingers against the metal railing. "Not so long ago, I was convinced I'd be alone all my life, too."

Too? Could Grace see more than Brooke had thought she was showing to those around her? Or was she simply basing her assessment on Brooke's own words, words she should have kept to herself?

"I know someone who has built a protective shell when I see one," Grace said. "I had a pretty thick one myself until Nathan slowly pecked away at it and made me believe in a bright future again."

Brooke leaned forward, intrigued. "How did he do that?"

"By gradually replacing bad memories with good ones."

Those words, the idea of them, soaked into Brooke like water trickling through rocks in a stream. "That sounds wonderful."

"It was, is. I still can't believe what a different person I am now than when I came here."

But Brooke was already a different person now, wasn't she? How many different incarnations could she have in one lifetime?

However many it took to be happy and safe again.

"Why are you telling me this? You barely know me."

"And yet I liked you the moment I met you." She smiled. "And I like Ryan. If you two were to get together, that would be wonderful for both of you. But that's up to no one but you two."

Brooke glanced back through the crowd, looking for Ryan. "I'm not sure—about anything." She redirected her attention to where the boat was drifting away from the dock. Why did she have to feel so mixed up inside? She'd come to Blue Falls in hopes of a life without drama, without complications, at least for a while.

Grace squeezed her hand. "You don't have to figure out whatever it is right this minute. Let things flow naturally. Maybe you'll just be good friends, nothing wrong with that." Grace paused for a couple of seconds. "Nothing wrong if it ends up being more, either." With that, Grace patted Brooke's hand and walked away, probably in search of her own handsome cowboy.

Nothing since she'd arrived at the Vista Hills Ranch felt quite real. Merline had welcomed her into her kitchen as if they'd been friends for years. Brooke had felt a connection with the youngest Teague brother from the moment they'd locked eyes, and everyone else—except perhaps Simon—thought that was grand. She shook her head as the wind off the water cooled her cheeks and lifted her hair. This kind of stuff didn't happen, not in real life. She fully expected to wake up to find it had all been an incredibly vivid dream.

She shivered. If she woke from this to find she was still in Virginia, still within Chris's grasp, she didn't think she could stand it.

"Cold?"

She jumped at the sound of Ryan's voice, but she hoped she covered it by shifting from one foot to the other. "A little cool. Hard to believe after how hot it's been."

"You haven't seen hot yet. Summer's still a month away."

"Then you all might be looking for another cook when I melt into a puddle of goo."

He leaned toward her from his spot next to the rail and spoke in a faux whisper. "We have this new-fangled thing called air-conditioning."

"Really? How progressive of you."

They fell into silence and watched as the sun dipped lower behind the hillside, casting a pinkish-orange glow across the surface of the water. The boat turned toward the waterfalls she'd only seen from a distance.

"It really is beautiful out here," she said.

"When we were kids, we used to come down here in the summer and jump into the lake from up there." Ryan pointed toward the top of the falls.

"That sounds like fun. We had a creek on our place growing up. My sister and I spent countless hours wading and chasing minnows."

"Where did you grow up?"

Brooke hesitated, more out of habit than any cautionary instinct about Ryan. "West Virginia."

"Long way from Texas."

In more ways than one.

Once they passed the falls, the announcement that dinner was ready saved her from further questions, if he had it in his mind to ask them.

He offered his arm. "Shall we?"

When she met the light in his eyes, one she hadn't seen in their short acquaintance, she couldn't say no. She slid her arm through his. As they walked toward the glass-enclosed dining area, for a moment she felt as if she was being led into some fancy ball on the arm of a handsome gentleman.

And she liked it.

RYAN WAS VERY much aware of the eyes on him and Brooke as he led her to the table and pulled her chair back for her, but he didn't acknowledge them. Maybe if he didn't act as though anything out of the ordinary was going on, he could pretend that he wasn't treading on dangerous ground.

But she'd been so beautiful standing out there in the glow of the sunset, her hair drifting in the breeze. She'd reminded him of the figureheads carved into the bows of old sailing ships.

He probably shouldn't have gone to stand with her,

to add to the speculation he could feel flowing through his family like a current. They didn't need to speak for him to hear their questions.

Did he like Brooke?

Would he ask her out?

Was this the thing that finally pulled him out of his self-imposed hermit status?

What everyone seemed to forget was that he hadn't exactly been the brother who tore up the dating circuit before he'd put on a uniform.

As he took his seat beside Brooke and listened to Amelia welcome everyone to the launch of a new season on the lake, he only half heard her. Most of his mind was focused on one question: was his attraction to Brooke just a natural reaction to his dry spell, or was more going on? Another question followed on that one's heels. If more was going on, did he want to saddle Brooke with a guy who was a bit of a time bomb, who never knew what might set off his post-traumatic stress disorder? One who had ugly things in his past.

For now, he liked being in her company. Maybe he'd just remember his former physical therapist's advice and take it one step at a time.

With her sitting next to him, he at least could keep himself from staring at her all night. If she'd been sitting across the table, he wasn't sure he'd have been able to say the same. And his mother would be imagining wedding bells again almost before Nathan and Grace's had stopped ringing.

"So, when do you think you're going to be able to play again?" Simon asked him from his seat on the other side of the table.

Ryan eyed his bandage. "Not sure. Week, maybe."

"Play?" Brooke asked.

He made the mistake of looking at her, getting stunned by the nearness of the woman who was short-circuiting his brain. "Uh, fiddle," he managed to mutter. He'd swear he heard muffled chuckles from his brothers, but he ignored them.

"We're in a band, the three of us," Nathan said, motioning between himself, Ryan and Simon.

"Really? What kind of music do you play?"

"Reggae," Simon said.

The confused look on Brooke's face caused everyone on their end of the table to laugh.

"Country, old and new," Ryan said.

"Well, that makes more sense," she said, prompting another round of laughs.

That laughter released some of the tension he hadn't fully been aware had built within him since the moment his mother had announced they were all spending the evening together on the boat. Gradually, it eased even more as the night went along and one conversation flowed into another. By the time the boat had docked at the end of the cruise, he was more relaxed than he'd been in a very long time.

"You seemed to have a nice time tonight," his mom said as everyone walked back to their vehicles.

"I did." He kept his answer simple, without much inflection.

She slowed beside him, forcing him to do so as well when she slipped her arm through his. "Any particular reason?"

He didn't have to look at her face to know she'd glanced several feet ahead to where Brooke was climbing into the back of the truck.

"Good food, good weather, good conversation."

His mom sighed a little. "I think she likes you."

"Mom, she barely knows me. And I barely know her. At best, we're friends."

"Friendship is a good place to start."

"Or stay."

Yes, he was wildly attracted to Brooke, but his mind was still way too muddled regarding her. He suspected if he ever gave in to that temptation that it wouldn't be like any time he'd gone on a date before. Something deep inside told him that one step down that road and the attraction would only grow.

They reached the truck before his mom could probe any further, and he held her hand as she lifted herself into her seat then slipped into his own.

Nobody talked much on the ride back to the ranch, and that was fine with him. He was content to stare out the window and replay all the laughs, smiles and words connected to Brooke throughout the cruise.

He'd gotten the sensation that he was watching the peeling back of a couple more layers, getting closer to the person Brooke really was. Because she was hiding something. He didn't have to be a cop like Simon to figure that much out. People didn't just up and move halfway across the country to a small town where they knew no one, had no place to stay and didn't even have a job if they were happy where they were.

If he hadn't had such a supportive and determined family, he wondered if he might have done the same thing after being discharged from the hospital and the army.

A buzzing sound came from the other side of the backseat. He looked over in time to see Brooke pull a phone from her purse. She clicked it to read a text message. He sensed more than saw her go rigid, but the fall of her loose hair hid her expression from him.

"Everything okay?" he asked.

She seemed to spring back into action, as if someone had paused her and now had hit the play button again. She dropped the cell back into her purse. "Yeah, just a message from my sister."

She shifted her attention out the window. She might only be tired, but his instincts were telling him it hadn't been a welcome message.

When they reached the ranch, he hated the idea of the night ending. But with his mom watching his every move, he squirmed at the idea of spending any more time with Brooke.

Until he saw the look on her face.

Chapter Eight

Chris called looking for you. I told him I didn't know where you were.

The text from Holly ruined what had been a lovely evening, slapping Brooke with the reason she was here in the first place. Why she couldn't get too close to anyone, no matter how much she might want to.

Brooke had never been afraid of the dark, not even as a child. But as she looked down the road she had to walk to reach the bunkhouse, an all-encompassing fear swamped her. It burrowed its way inside her mind and formed images of Chris lunging at her from the thick blackness of the trees. No amount of telling herself that the likelihood of Chris lurking in the shadows was minuscule managed to dispel the fear, and her legs refused to propel her forward. And she hated him all over again.

"Are you okay?" Ryan asked her, speaking low as though he didn't want his parents to hear. For that she was grateful.

"Yeah." She didn't know how she managed to voice the word when it felt like hands were crushing her throat, cutting off her air. But she made the mistake of looking up at him and saw that he knew she was lying.

"Good night," he said over his shoulder to his parents, then nodded slightly toward the road to the bunkhouse.

She knew it was weak, was frustrated with herself for needing it, but she grasped the lifeline and fell into step beside him.

Even with Ryan's strong presence next to her, she shivered a bit as they neared the trees. She had to get past this, because she couldn't exactly only come out during daylight hours like some sort of anti-vampire.

Something moved in the brush, and she yelped, backing up until she bumped into Ryan. His hands grasped her shoulders and steadied her. Embarrassed that she'd overreacted to what was likely no more than some animal scurrying through the bushes, she forced herself to calm down and step away from him. But even when she broke contact, she still felt the warmth of his hands lingering on her shoulders.

She scrambled for an excuse for her reaction, reminding herself that if Chris was calling Holly to try to find her then he obviously didn't know where she was. And wasn't hiding in the woods to jump out at her like the bogeyman.

"Sorry about that. Guess you can tell it's been a while since I've lived out in the country. I got too used to streetlights everywhere."

Hoping he wouldn't question her, she started walking again and resisted the irrational need to constantly check the layers of darkness along the road. Ryan didn't even mention the incident as they approached the bunkhouse. Instead, he walked up to her car and opened the back door.

"What are you doing?"

He shrugged those powerful shoulders of his. "I'm not the least bit tired. Might as well help you carry all this stuff in. You'll feel more at home when you've got your own things around."

She suspected there was more to his offer, that he was staying until she wasn't jumping at every little sound. In that case, she thought he might never leave. And a little voice somewhere inside her whispered that that wouldn't be such a bad thing.

Instead of declining his help as she might normally have done, she nodded. Truth was, she didn't want to be left alone right now. She needed at least a few minutes to get her head back on straight instead of allowing herself to fall victim to paranoia.

For the next several minutes they carried in boxes, plastic bins, bags and suitcases, emptying out all the car's various nooks and crannies. Once everything was stacked inside in piles, Ryan eyed it all.

"I can't believe all this was in that little car."

"Yes, I have perfected the art of bending space to my will."

He laughed and pointed toward a box. "You up for putting it all away?"

"You don't have to do that." She was inside without any reason for stepping back outdoors tonight. With a couple of locked doors, she thought she could make it through the night without having a freakout again.

"I know. But if I go back to my place, I'm just going to either stare at the ceiling or go out to the workshop. You wouldn't want me to get sleepy with dangerous tools in my hands, would you?" He gave her a teasing hint of a smile that was a little more like Simon but still somehow totally Ryan. For a moment, she wondered if he was hiding his real self, too. Why would he do that?

She remembered what she'd told herself mere minutes ago about not getting too close, but Ryan made sticking to that plan difficult. She had to believe she could cultivate a friendship without going too far.

"Well, if you put it that way," she said and tossed a pillow at him. "That goes on the couch."

He laughed as he caught the pillow with his good hand. The sound eased some more of her tension.

They worked well together. Gradually, she learned more about her new home—like the fact it had a washer and dryer where the breaker box was located.

"There's also a patio with a table, chairs and a grill out back," Ryan said.

"Really? I hadn't even looked yet."

A couple of hours passed before she realized that having a man in her home hadn't made her nervous. Either fate was telling her Ryan was safe to be around, or she was colossally stupid and didn't learn from her mistakes.

"Is this you?"

She looked over at the framed photo of her, Holly and their parents from when Brooke was seven and Holly twelve. "Yeah. And my sister." She stepped up beside him and pointed at Holly. "And Mom and Dad. We're at the New River Gorge."

"Near where you grew up?"

"About an hour away. I used to love going there."

"It's pretty."

"I haven't been there since my dad died. I guess I associate it with him too much." She had no idea why she'd shared that piece of herself, but it didn't feel wrong. It was inexplicably easy to talk to Ryan.

"He's been gone awhile?"

"He died when I was sixteen, in a mine cave-in." She bit her bottom lip for a moment as she took the photo from Ryan and stared at her parents. She still missed them every day. "He wasn't even supposed to work that day. He was filling in for a guy who had the flu."

"I'm sorry." The true compassion in his voice was almost her undoing, so she carried the photo across the room and placed it gently on a wall shelf.

"Bad things happen to good people," she said.

"Your mom's passed, too?"

"Yeah, four years ago from a stroke." She stared at the photo a moment longer before turning around and returning to work.

Thankfully, Ryan didn't ask her any more questions about her family. He was being so nice that she didn't want to be rude by not answering him or feel guilty for lying.

After a few more minutes, Ryan held up a sparkly crown. "You're secretly the queen of some tiny European country?"

She snorted. "I'll have you know I was Miss Whitcomb County. Keep digging and you'll find my sceptre."

"Don't take this the wrong way, but I didn't peg you for the beauty pageant type."

No, she'd been more the Beta Club and National Honor Society type, more at home watching *National Geographic Explorer* than hanging out at the mall.

"I did it on a dare. You know how there's always that one kid in school who rubs you the wrong way? Well, that was Camille Burns, who had an entire collection of those things." She pointed at the crown. "The only one she didn't have was the county pageant one. She wasn't exactly what you'd call modest, or nice for that matter. More of a spoiled twit. A friend of mine dared me to enter, more to irritate Camille than anything. I mean, she didn't need the scholarship money from those pageants like a lot of the other girls." Like Brooke. "Her daddy owned four KFC franchises. We called her the Chicken Princess."

"And you beat her."

Brooke smiled at the memory. "She squawked like one of the chickens her daddy was serving up every day."

"That I would have liked to have seen." He wiggled the crown. "And you parading around in this thing like royalty."

Feeling a giddiness that was as foreign as panic attacks had been before she'd figured out what kind of man Chris was, she strode over, took the crown and placed it on her head. She grabbed the sceptre from the box, assumed an aloof pose and tapped first one of his shoulders then the other.

"I knight thee Sir Ryan for valiant acts of woodworking and unpacking."

Ryan laughed. "I think you're getting punchy."

She pointed at him with the sparkly sceptre. "That is entirely possible." She tossed the sceptre back into the box but kept the crown on as they continued working. It made her feel good, took her back to days long before she knew her life would be torpedoed by a handsome man in an expensive suit.

After three hours on her feet, she collapsed onto the couch and noticed that it was nearing midnight. "You should go home. It's getting late."

"I'll go in a bit. I keep thinking I'm going to find a giant stash of Barbies."

Brooke laughed. "You're out of luck there. I gave them all to my nieces."

"Sure, shatter my hopes."

Brooke smiled as she leaned her head back against the couch and closed her eyes. "So, you know one of my embarrassing secrets. I think it's only fair you share one of yours."

"I don't have any."

"Hmm, maybe I'll just ask your mom."

"Now that's playing dirty."

She laughed and turned sideways on the couch to find him leaning against the kitchen counter. "You said you haven't been doing woodworking all that long. What were you into before that?"

"My brothers and I played football in high school."

"I thought all boys in Texas did that."

He gave her a scrunched-forehead look.

"Hey, I've seen *Friday Night Lights.*"

He pushed away from the counter and crossed the room to the comfortable chair perpendicular to the couch. When he sank into it, she thought she could see the long day was getting to him, too. "Football and horses, that was pretty much our lives back then."

"And music?"

It took him a moment to connect her question to their discussion about the band earlier. When he did, he laughed. "That was a prank that got out of hand."

"Oh, this sounds like a good story." She slid farther down the couch so that she was reclining against the piled pillows next to the arm.

"You know those family nights Mom enforces on Thursdays? Well, we thought if we put together a really terrible band, maybe she'd give them up. It backfired. She thought it was a great idea and bought us all instruments and lessons."

Brooke clapped her hands. "I love it."

"You sound like Grace."

She smiled at him. "It is pretty funny."

This time, he tossed a pillow at her. She laughed as she batted it away.

Though it was late and most of the work was done, Ryan didn't make any move to leave. But he didn't approach her either. He seemed content to simply sit and talk about everything from funny guests who had stayed at the ranch to her assertion that she would kill him at Trivial Pursuit.

She tried to keep her eyes open but they kept drifting shut. Each time it proved more difficult to open them again until finally she stopped trying. Instead, she focused on the rumble of Ryan's voice as it lulled her closer to sleep. He really did have the best voice. A sexy voice. A slow smile spread across her lips, and everything faded away.

QUIET DESCENDED ON the bunkhouse as Ryan stopped talking. From the sound of her slow, deep breathing, Brooke had finally fallen asleep. She looked so peaceful lying there on the couch, the slightest curve to her lips. His own sense of peace surprised him. A sliver of the person he used to be, the one who'd wanted nothing more than to protect others, fluttered to life.

He didn't know if there was a demon in her past or if she truly was just spooked by the thick night outside, but he found himself wanting to shield her from any threat, real or imagined. And that was dangerous ground to tread.

He dropped his head back against the chair and stared at the ceiling. Of all the people who came to the ranch, why was this woman messing with his equilibrium and his status quo?

Brooke shifted on the couch. When he returned his attention to her, she'd curled into a ball, as though she was trying to get warm. Likely to combat the daytime heat outside, she'd cranked the air-conditioning. Careful not to make too much noise, he stood and crossed to the thermostat. After adjusting it a couple of degrees, he returned and carefully used the blanket from the back of the couch to cover her. As he tucked it around her shoulders, he resisted the urge to also smooth her hair and run his fingertips along her soft cheek.

This woman he barely knew was bringing a part of him out of hibernation that he wasn't sure he was ready to confront. The part that wanted to live the life he might have had if things turned out differently during his tour of duty.

He shook his head and turned off the overhead light as he returned to the chair, leaving only the light over the sink to illuminate the room. He should probably leave, but he hated the idea of Brooke waking up and being scared. Of course he couldn't stay with her every night, but that didn't mean he couldn't give her some peace of mind tonight. If she woke, he'd be there to reassure her that nothing would harm her.

The combination of a long day, the sound of Brooke's deep breathing and the ticking of the clock on the wall lulled Ryan ever closer to sleep. He focused on Brooke's face—the curve of her jaw, the waves of her dark hair, the fan of her eyelashes. Knowing this might be the only time he'd be able to watch her like this without her noticing, he indulged until he too couldn't keep his eyes open and surrendered to sleep.

BROOKE WOKE TO a small click and the aroma of fresh-brewed coffee. It took a few seconds for sleep to recede enough for her to make sense of her surroundings. She was lying on the couch, a blanket draped over her. A blanket that hadn't been there the night before. She'd fallen asleep while talking to Ryan. The chair where he'd sat was empty, but she got the oddest sense that part of him lingered, as if he'd just left the room.

She lifted to a sitting position and put her feet on the floor. "Ryan?"

No answer.

The morning fog in her brain cleared a little more, and she spotted her crown on the coffee table. Ryan must have removed it when he placed the blanket over her. She hugged the blanket close, as if his scent or the comfort he brought her might be wrapped in its folds.

With the blanket around her shoulders, she went to the window and looked out just in time to see him rounding the corner in the drive that led into the stand of trees that had so frightened her the night before. He'd stayed with her all night. Her heart fluttered at the thought of him standing guard over her while she slept, keeping the night and her imagination at bay.

Remembering the cause for her fear the night before, she took out her phone and sent Holly a brief text. I'm sorry, but thank you. And then she forced herself to push Chris from her mind. A beautiful new day and memories of working alongside Ryan made that task easier than she expected.

She was going to have to tell herself Ryan had simply fallen asleep, too, or she was going to be in danger of falling for him no matter that common sense told her it was crazy.

But she'd think about all of that later. For now, she enjoyed a leisurely cup of coffee before getting ready for another day of work. Despite her determination not to think of Ryan in a romantic way, those were exactly the kinds of images that accompanied her as she show-

ered and dressed, as she walked through the no-longer-
scary trees to the main house. She even caught herself
whistling once as she cooked. More of her natural chat-
tiness came out as she talked with the guests who were
preparing to depart after their week at the ranch.

"I'm going to miss your cooking," said a computer
software programmer from California.

Brooke looked at the man's wife, worried that she
might be offended. The woman just shrugged.

"I agree with him," she said, which brought on a few
chuckles around the table.

The only thing that put any sort of dent in Brooke's
morning was the onset of a sudden nervousness when
she thought about seeing Merline again. The elder
Teagues had seen her walk off into the night with Ryan,
and she could only imagine what they must be thinking.

She needn't have worried, however. When Merline
entered the house midmorning after working a couple
of hours at the gallery, she was on her cell phone and
distracted.

"That's terrible. What are you going to do?"

Brooke busied herself with some prep work for lunch
and added a few items to the grocery list, but by the end
of Merline's phone conversation her curiosity was demanding satisfaction.

"Is everything okay?"

Merline looked up as she placed her cell on the
island. "My best friend's daughter is getting married
next weekend, and the church where they were getting
married had a fire last night."

"Oh, no. Was anyone hurt?"

"No, it was the middle of the night, so it was empty.
But she's desperate to find another place on short notice
and isn't having any luck."

"What about here?"

"Here?"

"Yeah, you could get one of those arches and set it up in that pretty meadow on the way into the ranch. Then we could do the reception here at the house. I'm sure the ranch guests wouldn't mind. You could rent one of those portable dance floors and have dancing outside by the picnic tables if the weather is nice." A smile tugged at the edges of Brooke's mouth. "Even have your sons provide the music."

Merline placed her palms against Brooke's cheeks in a gesture of affection. "I think I'm going to adopt you. That idea is so perfect, I don't know why I didn't think of it. Let me talk to Annabelle. If she says yes, we'll get to work."

A familiar warmth flowed through Brooke. This was the thing she missed about her job in D.C., the coming up with solutions to help people prepare the perfect event. Weddings and receptions had been among her favorite events to coordinate. Way more exciting than a conference full of building-supply salespeople.

A few minutes later, Merline returned beaming. "She loved the idea. They're going to come over from Austin this afternoon to make plans. They have caterers already, but I'd like to give everyone a little something special, a little Vista Hills flavor. Any ideas?"

A surge of pride welled up in Brooke that Merline was consulting her on something so important, that she valued her opinion.

"I could make some hand-dipped chocolates, decorate them with the wedding colors."

"Perfect. I know her main color is a bright orange, very striking."

They sketched out some ideas to present to Annabelle and her daughter, Adrienne, when they arrived.

"Well, I need to get some ranch work done before they get here," Merline said half an hour later.

"Is there anything I can help you with?"

"You've already saved the day. What else could I ask for?"

Little did Merline know these types of suggestions weren't much of a stretch for Brooke. She'd made dozens, hundreds of similar ones in consultation with the rest of the staff at the hotel and countless outside vendors. But it still felt good to be appreciated for her talents. To be allowed a taste of what she'd left behind.

Merline started to leave, but Brooke needed an answer to a question she'd been mulling all morning.

"Merline?"

"Yes."

"Ryan was kind enough to help me unload my car last night." She forced herself not to fidget as she continued. "I thought I might make something to thank him and was wondering what his favorite dessert is."

Merline smiled but looked as if she was keeping an even bigger smile from forming. "Macaroons. That boy has always been crazy for macaroons. I used to make them for him when he was overseas, a little taste of home. They were so popular that I had to send bigger and bigger boxes of them so he could share them with his buddies."

"He was in the military?"

The look of fond memory faded from Merline's face, as if she realized she'd said something she hadn't meant to. She hesitated a moment before answering. "Yes, the army." She made to leave again. "Macaroons will definitely make his day."

After Merline left, Brooke considered the odd change in the other woman. Maybe she was just remembering how she'd missed her son while he was serving, maybe how she'd worried about him. Brooke was pretty sure she'd have a fifty-fifty chance of guessing where he'd been stationed while out of the country.

As she made the macaroons, Brooke argued with herself about whether she was making a mistake. Was she truly just doing this to thank him for his help, or was it an excuse to see him, to get closer? She was acting against every promise she'd made to herself the day she'd driven out of Arlington for the last time.

Then why did it feel right?

She shook her head as she placed the finished macaroons in a tin she found in the cabinet under the island. She had to stop overthinking everything she did or she was going to drive herself batty.

With a new resolve to let life unfold how it would, she popped a macaroon in her mouth and headed to Ryan's place.

When she arrived, she heard him on the phone in the house so she decided to wait in his shop. Inside, she eyed the various projects in different states of completion, running her fingers over the carved designs Ryan had brought to life out of simple wood. As she reached the end of the workbench, something new caught her attention.

Brooke lifted a piece about eight inches tall, an intricately carved angel with outspread wings, long hair and waving robes. It was hard to believe something so delicate had been made by human hands.

"Brooke?"

She looked up as Ryan entered the workshop. "This is beautiful."

A momentary shock registered on his face before he strode forward and took the angel from her. "It's nothing, just something I do to pass the time when I can't sleep."

"You've made others?"

"A few." He stared at the angel for a couple of seconds before shoving it to the back of a shelf.

"You should make more, maybe sell those in the shops in town."

"No."

Brooke took an unintentional step backward at the firmness in his answer.

"I'm sorry," he said. "It's just that they're...personal."

She nodded. "Okay." She wanted to know so much more, but it wasn't her right to push.

"What's that?" Ryan nodded at the tin in her hands.

She extended it toward him. "A thank-you for your help last night."

He accepted the tin. "This wasn't necessary."

"It was to me. I really appreciate the help and...thank you for staying." Heat rose up her neck as she wondered how he'd take her thank-you and gift.

"You're welcome. You okay today?"

"Yes, thank you. I, uh, I have panic attacks sometimes." She tensed, hoping he didn't ask why.

He didn't. Instead, he opened the tin. "Macaroons." He sounded surprised.

"Your mom said they were your favorite."

"They are, but I haven't had them in a while." He hesitated for a moment before lifting one of the macaroons to his mouth and taking a bite. He made a deep, appreciative sound that made her tingle all over. "Don't tell her, but these are even better than my mom's."

She smiled at the high praise. "Yeah, in the name

of job security, I think I'll keep that little nugget to myself."

Ryan offered to share, so she took another treat for herself. "How's your hand today?"

"Good. Beginning to heal."

"How long before you think you can play your fiddle?"

"I don't know really. A few days at least. Why?"

"Because we're having a wedding here at the ranch next weekend, and I volunteered your band as the reception entertainment."

"What? Why'd you do that? We could stink for all you know."

"Do you?"

He braced his hands against the edge of the workbench. "Well, no. We're decent."

She walked up next to him and gave him a friendly pat on the shoulder. "Then you'd better be picking out some good dancing tunes."

"You're going to owe me more macaroons for this."

She laughed. "How about I just give you a hand around here for a little bit, and we'll call everything even?"

"That's a start."

Chapter Nine

Ryan clamped down on the crazy thought that he should demand a kiss as payment, but he didn't want to scare Brooke away. Though she seemed happy and carefree now, last night had been a different story. Her revelation about having panic attacks might be true, but there was more to it. She'd been really frightened by the darkness—or what she'd feared was in it. He'd wanted nothing more than to protect her, to make sure she was safe.

But he wasn't the right person for that job, was he? He couldn't believe he needed reminding of that fact. Still, something about her made him want to believe he could be that man again. The one who'd gone off to war with high ideals of making a difference in the world. It was easy being with her, something he couldn't say about anyone else. Of course, she was the only person who didn't know about what he'd done.

It caused an uncomfortable tightening in his chest, but he had to back away. Maybe someday they could be easy friends, but for now he couldn't risk being around her, tempting him into wanting more.

Ryan slipped a spindle onto the back of a chair. "Thanks for your help," he said with a brief glance at Brooke. "That's all I need for now. I've got an appointment in town."

"Oh," Brooke said, her eyes widening a little at his abrupt shift in gears.

"And thanks again for the macaroons." He gave her a nod then headed for his truck, fully aware he was running like a scared little kid.

When he got to town, he sat at the stoplight and tried to figure out what to do next. He didn't actually have any errands to run, nothing to deliver, and he wasn't in the mood to chat it up with any of his family members. If it was later in the day, he'd hit the Frothy Stein for a beer. But even as messed up as he was, he wasn't going to start drinking before lunch.

Lunch. Maybe he'd just grab something to eat at the Wildflower Café while he attempted to get his head on straight and stop thinking like a giant walking hormone.

But when he stepped in the front door of the café a couple of minutes later, he regretted not heading for that beer after all. It was too late to retreat though. Simon had already seen him and waved him over to his table in the front corner.

Damn, why hadn't he just gotten a sandwich at the Qwik Stop and gone to sit by the lake?

Because even the lake reminded him of Brooke.

"What are you doing in town?" Simon asked as Ryan pulled out a chair and sank into it.

"Came to check on the stock." He winced inside as soon as he said it. He never came to the shops in town to see when they needed any new items from him. They always did the calling.

"That's new." Damn Simon for looking like he knew something else was going on.

Ryan lifted his injured hand. "Might as well do something productive while this heals."

"Your helper go AWOL?"

"Brooke has her own job." Why had he ever let her help him in the first place? He was just asking for trouble, for unwanted comments from his family. He'd had a nice, quiet life, nothing unexpected—until she'd come along.

Ryan ordered a burger and onion rings and tried to figure out a way to steer the conversation in a different direction.

"Mom says we're playing at Adrienne and Riley's wedding this weekend," Simon said.

"So I heard."

"Also heard it was Brooke's idea, and that she seemed excited when she'd suggested it."

She had?

Ryan met his brother's gaze. "If you're getting at something, just spit it out and quit beating around the bush."

"When are you going to ask that woman out?"

"I'm not."

"Why? It's obvious you're crazy about her."

He thought about denying it, but his brother wasn't one to be easily fooled. "You know why."

"I know what you think is a reason."

Ryan leaned forward. "No woman in her right mind is going to want to be with someone who did what I did."

"You mean defend innocent people?"

Ryan's fists clenched involuntarily. "It's not that simple."

"No, it's not. But you can't let what happened ruin the rest of your life."

"My life is fine."

"Your life is empty."

Ryan leaned back and shook his head. "You're one

to talk. I don't see you following in Nathan's footsteps, settling down and contributing a couple of kids to the family tree."

"Who said anything about settling down? I was just suggesting you ask Brooke out on a date." Simon's knowing expression, confident that he'd gotten Ryan to admit more than he'd intended, grated Ryan's nerves.

"I thought you had the hots for her anyway."

"I know a pretty woman when I see one."

"Then *you* ask her out." Ryan knew he sounded exasperated, but he just didn't care anymore. Maybe if Simon hooked up with Brooke, he could go back to the way things were.

Yeah, right.

"Maybe I will." Simon tossed some cash on the table and stood. "Enjoy your lunch."

Ryan gritted his teeth as Simon strode out of the café, tipping his hat at every woman between their table and the door. Didn't matter whether they were seven or seventy-seven, they all smiled and fell for his charm. Ryan sighed. Even before he'd gone and gotten himself messed up physically and mentally, he hadn't possessed his older brother's swagger. It just wasn't in him. If Simon decided to really go for Brooke, Ryan didn't stand a chance.

When his burger and onion rings arrived, he couldn't even enjoy them. They tasted too much like failure.

BROOKE THREW HERSELF into the plans for the wedding, working with Adrienne on an extended menu. The Austin caterers were still involved with the more formal reception, but Adrienne and Riley also wanted some offerings more in keeping with the ranch, the place where they'd met and fallen in love. Plus, the party was going to go long into the night with the dancing, and everyone would need more than cake and finger foods.

Brooke found herself even tossing in ideas about the ceremony itself, glad to have something positive on which to focus her thoughts and energy. At first it felt awkward each time Merline consulted her, but her boss seemed determined to enlist her help in more than cooking. She even asked her to start taking bookings for the cabins when Merline was away from the ranch. Unable to help herself, Brooke had scribbled down some ideas for additional guest services and ways to get the word out about Vista Hills.

"I do hope you know you can never leave," Merline said Thursday morning as she enjoyed her second cup of coffee while Brooke kneaded dough for homemade pizzas. "I don't know what I ever did without you."

Brooke smiled. "It's not so much."

"Not so much? I feel like I got a cook, a guest relations manager and a PR person all in one."

That hit too close to the truth. "So, Adrienne said that she wasn't satisfied with what the bakery in Austin was coming up with for the groom's cake. Have you heard if she's let them go?"

"Yeah. They make beautiful wedding cakes, but for some reason can't manage a decent groom's cake. Doesn't make any sense at all."

"So we'll need one of those, too."

"We got it taken care of. Keri Mehler in town is making it. That girl has a real knack for cakes. If we'd known the wedding was going to be out here from the beginning, Annabelle would have had her make the wedding cake."

"Oh."

"Nothing against you, sweetie, but you've got a lot on your to-do list already."

Not enough to keep her so busy she didn't have time to wonder what she'd done or said to push Ryan away. Since she'd taken him the macaroons, he'd steered clear of her, not asking for help and not coming up to the main house for meals. She'd kicked herself at least a dozen times for being a fool again. Except this time, the man wasn't trying to consume her. He was running as fast as he could the other way. It was just more proof that she didn't have the slightest talent in reading men and should stop trying.

That made her feel incredibly alone, no matter that the ranch was always busy with people coming and going.

She managed to fill the time that she wasn't performing her actual job and working on the wedding planning with making the bunkhouse feel more like her space, going for a long hike on one of the ranch trails, and getting a P.O. box in town. After ensuring Chris couldn't follow the U.S. Postal Service right to her front door, she still didn't feel any better. It'd been four days since she'd spoken to Ryan. What kind of sense did it make to miss someone you barely knew?

Instead of heading straight back to the ranch after the post office, she wandered through some of the shops in town, admiring the handmade crafts from pottery to quilts, from photography to…she stopped and stared. There in the corner of a shop called the Blue Falls Bazaar, she spotted a small, round table made by Ryan. She'd know those carved flower petals anywhere. Before she could talk herself out of it, she'd forked over enough cash to make it hers. As she carried it out to her car, she called herself a hundred kinds of fool. She could try convincing herself she simply admired the crafts-manship, but it felt like wasted effort.

Once inside her car, she sat staring out the wind-shield. This was silly. He'd done her a favor. His pulling back was a necessary wake-up call that she had other things to focus on, and romance shouldn't even be a blip on the radar. She reordered her thoughts, approaching the situation from a different angle. When she saw him, she had to think of him as an employer, albeit a very nice-looking one, and nothing more. She kept repeating her new plan in her head all the way back to the ranch.

"Oh, good, you're back," Merline said as Brooke entered the kitchen an hour later with a bag of groceries. "Thought you were going to miss all the fun."

Brooke eyed Merline and Grace, who appeared to be making grilled-cheese sandwiches at the stove.

"Fun?"

"Family night," Merline said. "Thursday, remember?"

Brooke racked her memory for some snippet of conversation she'd missed. "I'm sorry, did I forget to do something?"

"No. It's Grace's night to host."

"I just got a Wii for Evan, so we're going to play Wii bowling," Grace said.

Their intent snapped into place. Brooke put away the last of the groceries in the refrigerator, trying to figure out the least offensive way to make her point. "When you had hands living in the bunkhouse, did they take part in family night?"

Grace gave Merline a meaningful glance, something that had a hint of "I told you so."

"No."

"Then why invite me?"

"Well, you're different."

Brooke swallowed. "No, I'm not. I appreciate the kind offer, but this night is reserved for your family. And I'm not family." She wanted to say more, to wish them a good night and that she'd see them in the morning, but she didn't think she could speak any more without giving her heartache away.

She walked out the back door, blinking against the stupid tears that didn't have any right to form. Saying those words, that she wasn't family, shouldn't have hurt so much.

But it did.

Needing some connection to her own family, she dialed Holly's number as she headed back to the bunkhouse. When Holly answered, Brooke nearly cried.

"Hey, sis," Brooke said.

"Brooke. Oh, I'm so glad to hear from you. Are you okay?"

"Yes, fine. Just missing you all a bit."

"We miss you, too. How are things there?"

"Nice. Good people, I like the job." She was surprised by how much truth was in that assertion. It was so different from the career she'd built for herself, but that didn't make her like it any less.

The sound of children's voices rose in the background, drowning out whatever Holly was saying in response. Brooke smiled as Holly's voice faded a bit as she talked to her daughters. This was such a normal part of their conversations that Brooke's heart lifted.

"Emma is dying to talk to you," Holly said.

"Okay, put her on."

"Hi, Aunt Brooke!"

"Hi, yourself. What are you doing?"

"Making cookies!" Everything was always high excitement with her youngest niece. But then maybe everything was really exciting when you were four years old.

"Oh, yum. What kind?"

"I don't know."

Brooke laughed. "Okay, we'll just call them mystery cookies."

"Mystery cookies!"

Brooke laughed again and wished she could wrap Emma in her arms. She prayed she felt safe enough to do that soon. "Let me say hello to your sister."

"Okay." Emma, satisfied with her few words of conversation, handed over the phone.

"Hey, Aunt Brooke. They're actually chocolate chip cookies," seven-year-old Caitlyn said in that frustrated, superior way of older sisters.

After a few minutes of talking about the approaching end of the school year and one more contribution from Emma—"I'm adding sprinkles!"—Holly reclaimed the phone.

"Sprinkles on chocolate chip cookies, huh?"

"Yes, we do avant-garde cookies here."

Brooke smiled wide. "I'm so glad I called."

"Me, too. I hate that you're so far away." She was careful not to say a location, not wanting the girls to hear and possibly let it slip at the wrong time in front of the wrong person.

Though hopefully Chris and the girls would never cross paths. It was bad enough that he'd called Holly.

"Hey, at least I didn't up and jet off to Australia. That was looking pretty attractive. I mean, they do have Hugh Jackman in their favor."

Holly was the one to laugh this time. "I'd have to hate you for that. I'd give up Clay for Hugh Jackman."

"I heard that," Holly's husband, Clay, said from the background.

"Just kidding," Holly said, laughter evident in her voice. "How could I ever leave the King of the Dairy Cows?"

After several more minutes of catching up, they ended the call. The improved mood lasted until Brooke looked around her at the inside of the bunkhouse, at the fact that she was alone here.

That aloneness felt more acute now that she'd had contact with her family. Now that Ryan had decided he wanted nothing to do with her.

CONSIDERING HOW poor-pitiful-me she'd felt for the past week, Brooke woke up Saturday morning in a good mood. Maybe it was the sun rising on another beautiful day, or the fact she'd been able to talk to her sister and nieces, or perhaps the fact that two people were going to start their happily-ever-after today. Whatever the reason, she was glad for it. She was done with mooning over a guy who didn't have any interest in her. If she found someone again someday, great. If not, she'd be okay.

Besides, she didn't have time to think about Ryan Teague today.

The kitchen of the main house buzzed with activity from the moment she stepped in, Merline and Grace helping her prepare everything for their part of the reception. Midmorning, Keri Mehler arrived from the bakery with the groom's cake, and Brooke went out to help her carry it in. She tripped on her own foot when she rounded the corner of the house and spotted Ryan headed into the barn with his brothers. She jerked her gaze away, but not before Keri noticed.

"Girlfriend, no matter which one you're looking at, you're asking for a heap of trouble."

The comment surprised her, but she couldn't say she disagreed with Keri.

When Keri opened the back of her delivery van, Brooke gasped. "It's gorgeous." The three-tier chocolate cake was a masterpiece of edible art with handcrafted lonestars in a bright orange ringing the outsides and a miniature version of the ranch on top.

Keri stood back with her hands on her hips. "I do think I outdid myself this time."

They got the cake safely inside, and Brooke went back to work, trying to forget how that momentary glimpse of Ryan had made her heart jolt in her chest.

When everyone finally went off to get dressed for the ceremony, she collapsed into a chair. She was still sitting there when Merline and Hank walked into the kitchen dressed in their wedding finery.

"You're not dressed," Merline said.

"I brought something to change into. I'll be ready by the time everyone gets here."

"You're not going to the ceremony?"

"No, I have a few more things to do here." She didn't think she could bear to watch two people so in love when her attempts had proved so disastrous.

Merline looked as though she might say something more, but Hank gently guided her out the door with a slight nod in Brooke's direction, as if he understood.

For several long minutes, she simply sat and enjoyed the quiet before the festivities moved back to the house and the portable dance floor that had been set up outside. Though she shouldn't, she allowed herself to imagine, just for a moment, what it would be like to dance in the circle of Ryan's arms.

She shook off the image and scolded herself. When the clock hit the appointed time, she started setting the food out on the guest dining room's sideboard and tables. She placed a small box of handmade chocolates at every seat. She reserved several boxes for the guests who chose to sit outside so that their chocolate wouldn't melt in the heat. She finished changing into her blue silk dress and silver slingbacks and pulled her hair up into a twist just before the first guests started arriving.

Dressed as she was, surrounded by people, directing traffic, she felt more like her old self than she had in a long time. And it felt really, really good.

When Ryan stepped in the dining room's exterior door, he stopped, nearly causing a couple behind him to walk right into his back. He sidestepped then met her eyes; what she saw in his made butterflies spring to fluttering life in her stomach. That wasn't the look of an uninterested man, was it? Could she be so totally off base not to recognize what she believed was staring back at her?

He seemed to realize he was openly staring and broke eye contact. A middle-aged man she didn't recognize started talking to him as they flowed into the food line. Someone stepped close to her side.

"If you're trying to not draw Ryan's interest, I don't think that dress was the right move."

Brooke touched the front of her dress and looked down at the shimmery fabric. Before she could think how to respond, Grace stepped away with a wink and a knowing smile back at Brooke.

Brooke retreated to the kitchen and quite frankly hid there until Ryan and most of the guests had filled their plates and made their way to the tables outside.

She half expected Merline or Grace to come find

her, but they left her alone. After a couple of minutes, she felt silly and straightened. She'd made the food, so she was going to enjoy it. Evan spotted her first as she stepped outside with her plate and waved wildly at her to come sit by him. She smiled wide and slipped into the empty chair. She leaned close to Evan.

"So, are you going to save me a dance?" she asked.

He fiddled with his fork. "I'm not a very good dancer."

"I bet you're better than you think."

After she ate and chatted with her tablemates for a few minutes, Brooke got back to work collecting trash. The rest of the Teagues lent a hand so that the task didn't take very long. As she returned from her last trip to the trash bins inside the dining room's utility closet, Ryan's band launched into the notes of the first song. She watched as Riley led Adrienne to the dance floor and pulled her into his arms. They looked so perfect together, so in love.

She stuck to the shadows as night began to fall, at the edge of the light cast by the ropes of hanging lights draped around the dance floor. But when she spotted Evan sitting by himself, watching his parents and the rest of the adults dance, she remembered their earlier conversation. Weaving among the tables, she made her way to him.

"I believe you owe me a dance."

He hesitated a moment, looked at his dad, whom he obviously worshipped, and slid out of his seat. He took her hand and led her to the dance floor as he'd watched so many others do all night.

"Now, see, you are a good dancer," she said once they'd made one circuit of the floor.

"Really?"

"One of the best here."

He beamed as if she'd paid him the highest of compliments.

They finished out the song, the last in the band's first set. Nathan announced they'd be back in a few minutes, and recorded music was put on for those not wanting to leave the dance floor. Brooke had taken one step to leave when Evan stopped her.

"I think my uncle wants to dance with you."

Her heart rate picked up, and she couldn't decide whether to hurry to the safety of the house or act as if nothing was out of the ordinary. No, she was done running, right? She squeezed Evan's hand, thanked him for the dance and turned to face…Simon.

Chapter Ten

Not for the first time, Ryan wondered if he'd lost his mind, left it behind in that Iraqi village. Because what kind of sense did the feelings roiling inside him make? The ones that made his jaw clench and his hands curl into fists as he watched Simon pull Brooke into his arms and spin her around the dance floor. How could he feel something so powerful for a woman he'd known less than two weeks?

Yeah, he was definitely crazy.

But she did look stunning tonight. When he'd first seen her in that blue dress, her hair swept up to reveal the delicate skin of her neck, his heart and lungs had momentarily forgotten how to function. He doubted a good jolt of electricity could have stunned him any more.

Brooke laughed at something Simon said, and Ryan cursed himself for urging his brother to ask Brooke out. Because that was where this night was going.

Not if he could help it.

Before he could talk himself out of it, he started across the temporary dance floor, intent that if anyone was going to hold Brooke in his arms and make her laugh, it was going to be him.

When he got close to Brooke and Simon, his brother

stepped back as if he'd been expecting him all along. For a moment, Ryan felt like he'd been tricked onto the dance floor, but one glance at Brooke and he didn't care.

"Looks like it's time to share," Simon said before kissing Brooke's hand. As he turned to leave, Simon gave Ryan one of those annoying smiles he'd perfected as a young boy. The one that said, "I maneuvered you to get my way."

He ignored Simon, turned to Brooke and held out his hand. Her smile looked nervous, so when she placed her hand in his he grasped it with a firm grip, one he hoped was reassuring. He wanted her nervousness to fade when she was with him, wanted her to enjoy dancing with him.

Gently, he placed his other hand on her back and drew her close, his eyes locked with hers the entire time. She broke eye contact first, so he pulled her a step closer. For a moment, he closed his eyes and enjoyed the feel of her soft, warm curves. It'd been so long since he'd held a woman like this, and he'd somehow convinced himself he didn't miss it.

What a lie.

"You all are good," she said with a slight nod toward the stage.

"At least we don't make dogs howl and small children cry."

"Deflecting praise again. You do that a lot."

"Do I?"

"Yes."

It wasn't intentional. Or was it?

"You're talented," she said. "Multitalented. And I'm not the only one to notice."

But at the moment, she was the only one who mattered. "Thank you."

She smiled, making him feel as though he was basking in a beam of sunlight. "Now, see, that wasn't so hard."

The song ended, but he didn't release her, instead he led her into the next song. She didn't seem to mind.

So gradually he didn't realize it was happening, she moved closer to him with each dance step until only a sliver of space separated their bodies. Ryan inhaled the scent of roses, and his pulse quickened. He wanted this woman so much he thought he might burst with the wanting. By the way she moved, her head so close to lying on his shoulder, he'd swear she was feeling the same way.

"Brooke?"

"Yes?"

"Would you like to leave?"

It took an agonizing moment for her to answer, but it was worth the wait. She looked up at him with a hint of that nervousness again, but a lot more of what he hoped was desire. He didn't want to be the only one feeling this flush with a thrumming need to touch and be touched.

"Yes."

Not caring that the band was due back up on the stage any minute, he led her from the dance floor. His brothers would just have to play songs that didn't require a fiddle.

EVERY NERVE ENDING in her hand where Ryan held it sizzled like a Fourth of July sparkler. As he led her away from the lights and sounds of the party, she grew more jittery—not out of fear, but of anticipation and a fervent hope that she wasn't making a mistake.

At some point while they danced, she'd felt an absolute certainty that Ryan was a good man, as different from Chris as white was from black, slip into place inside her. No, it wasn't any fear of Ryan that had her nervous. It was allowing herself to feel too much when she might have to leave someday if Chris ever found her.

Ryan didn't speak as he led her toward his home. He didn't walk too fast, likely out of deference to her shoes, but she wanted to throw them off so they could reach their destination sooner. With each step the desire to turn him toward her and kiss him silly built inside her.

At the end of the short driveway to his house, Ryan suddenly turned. "I want to kiss you." He was breathless, as if he'd been holding in those words along with his breath. And he looked a touch surprised that what he'd been thinking had actually tumbled out of his mouth.

By way of answer, she moved toward him and lifted her hand to rest against his cheek.

Ryan wrapped his strong arms around her and lowered his lips to hers. If the simple touch of his hand was like sparklers, his kiss was nothing short of fireworks over D.C.—hot, powerful, full of brilliant colors that made her heart sing.

She slid her hands to the back of his neck, then into his hair. Without thinking about it, she lifted onto her toes to bring herself even closer to him. He tasted like chocolate cake and smelled like pine-scented soap, and she was overtaken with the thought that she couldn't get enough of him.

He broke the kiss but not the contact everywhere else. "Are you okay?"

She nearly cried at his honest concern, at the memory that Chris had never asked her that. How stupid she'd been for not noticing, for thinking his lack of concern had just been his way of acknowledging she was a strong woman.

"Brooke?"

She smiled. "Yes." She looked up at him, his face in partial shadow, and wondered if she'd ever get enough of the sight of those angles and curves. "More than okay."

After another lingering kiss, Ryan took her hand again and led her the rest of the way up the lane.

Once inside his house, he didn't turn on the lights. "I've never brought anyone here."

The admission touched her, and this time she initiated a kiss herself. His hands slid down her bare arms to her lower back. She could feel not only the strong muscles in his arms and chest but also what all this kissing and caressing was doing to him in other places.

Considering what she'd been through, being alone with a man in this position could have scared her. But it didn't. In fact, she wanted even more of Ryan Teague, whatever he was willing to give.

Ryan backed up until he bumped the couch, then sank onto it. Without ending the kiss, he guided Brooke between his powerful legs. The legs of a horseman, a soldier.

The surge of desire that his kiss brought out in her was so powerful it made her shake.

Ryan pulled back. "Too much?"

Not enough.

"It's..." She swallowed, determined not to let Chris ruin her new life, too. "It's been a while since..."

Ryan ran his fingers along the edge of her jaw. "I won't hurt you."

"I know." The words pushed past the lump in her throat as a whisper.

"Whoever he was, he was a fool."

She tensed.

"You don't have to tell me anything."

"I…" Her words faltered halfway between saying nothing and telling him every horrible detail. "I was with someone who…" She swallowed hard, and Ryan took her hand in his, squeezed it. Despite a desire to be honest, she couldn't force the truth out into the open. She couldn't risk it. "Let's just say I have a less than awesome dating record." She forced a self-deprecating smile as if what she'd gone through had been no more than the realization she was dating a jerk.

A fire flashed in Ryan's eyes, perhaps a hint of the soldier he'd once been, before he doused it. She feared she hadn't hidden enough, that the truth had somehow shown in her eyes.

"Well, anyone you were with before isn't here now," he said. "I am." He kissed her again, this time so soft and gentle that the tenderness nearly made her cry.

He was right. Chris wasn't here. Instead, she was wrapped in the arms of a strong but kind, quiet and passionate man. A man who made her skin tingle and her heart tap dance.

"Ryan?" she said against his lips.

"Yeah?"

"Do you…could we go to your bedroom?"

Amazement registered on his face that mirrored what she felt inside. She might not have known him long, might have promised herself not to trust again so soon, but something about being with Ryan just felt right.

He seemed as without words as she was when he took her hand and backed toward his room, refusing to look away from her, as if she were some rare and beautiful flower. If she knew every flattering adjective ever created, she'd be unable to describe how the look in his eyes made her feel.

He left the light in his bedroom off, for which she was grateful. She loved looking at him, but she was afraid she'd think too much if what they were about to do was exposed to full light. What shined in from the living room was enough to see how to release the first button on his shirt.

Ryan laid his hand over hers, stopping her. "Are you sure about this? We haven't known each other long."

"Does this feel wrong to you?"

"No." The certainty in his answer heartened her, gave her more confidence to continue unbuttoning his shirt.

She was halfway down the row, giving her a glimpse of his naked chest beneath, when he stopped her with another kiss. This one, however, burned with more fire and she found herself being guided slowly toward the bed. As he laid her back onto the cool sheets, she managed to thoroughly enjoy the kiss while also finishing with the buttons. She spread the shirt wide and placed her palms against his smooth chest.

Ryan's sudden intake of air made her smile against his lips.

"Flirt." His voice was raspy and deep, laced with a promise she really wanted him to keep.

Feeling bold, she nipped at his bottom lip. He growled and slid his hands up her arms to clasp her hands above her head. The succession of kisses that followed left her feeling like a bowl of noodles.

"I think I've discovered another of your talents," she said as he kissed her neck.

"There's more," he said next to her ear, making her shiver in a very, very good way.

"Promises, promises," she teased, hardly recognizing herself.

"Promises I intend to keep."

He drugged her with endless kisses to her lips, her ears, her neck as he unzipped her dress and carefully pulled it over her head. And then he set those magnificent lips to work on the swell of her breasts above her bra. She gasped and arched into him. The top edge of her bra edged down, granting him access to more sensitive skin.

She wanted to tell him to just take it off, but she couldn't form words. But she didn't have to. He seemed to read her mind, slipping his hands beneath her to unsnap her bra. With a wicked grin, he pulled it off and tossed it on top of the discarded dress.

With hungry fingers, she shoved his open shirt off his shoulders. When it joined the party of discarded clothing, she couldn't get enough of running her hands over his warm, taut flesh. The muscles in his back made her mouth water, and she lifted slightly to kiss his chest. Getting hotter with each passing moment, she let inhibition float away and licked his right nipple.

His body went rigid above her, followed quickly by a growl and then a demanding kiss. Ryan was no doubt strong, but his strength and power in this situation only served to fan the flames growing inside her. She met his deep kiss, pouring all of herself into it. The urgency built between them like a living thing, and their grasping hands made short work of the final barriers between them—his pants and underwear and her panties.

She suffered a moment of panic, but it was quickly replaced with screaming desire as Ryan grasped her hips and rained kisses from her neck to her stomach.

He lifted himself so he could look down at her then cradled her face in his hand. "I never expected this."

"Me, neither," she said, trying to catch her breath.

"But I like it."

She smiled. "Me, too."

"Will you let me make love to you?"

"Ryan, the way I'm feeling right now, I might beg you to."

With another growl that made her entire body vibrate, he captured her mouth in another deep kiss as he gently spread her legs. The tip of him pressed against her, and she was done with waiting. She lifted herself against him, and he pushed fully inside. He paused only for a moment, letting her body accommodate him, before he started to move.

Her entire world became the sensation of him sliding in and out of her center, and her breathing came faster and faster, urging his pace to increase. She gripped his hips and met each of his thrusts. Faster, deeper, faster, deeper. Her breath caught as she felt the beginnings of release starting to build at that hidden place within her. She focused on that tightening of inner muscles, the slick feel of Ryan, the ragged, hungry sound of his breathing as he rocked against her. Oh, she was getting closer...and closer...and closer.

With one final burst of energy propelling her upward, she took him as deep as she could and let go of a spasming release. He followed her lead and stiffened as he found his own.

Spent, Ryan collapsed beside her but still had enough energy to pull her into his arms. She snuggled next to his chest and listened as his heartbeat gradually slowed from the thundering pace their lovemaking had set.

"That was…" He continued to breathe in full gulps of air.

"Wonderful." She said it softly, but he heard her because he gently squeezed her closer and kissed the top of her head.

After a few beats of silence, he said, "Yeah. Wonderful." His words sounded slow, languid, sleepy. And she found she felt much the same.

Her eyes drifted shut, more relaxed than she could ever remember feeling. Safer. She tried to resist sleep, afraid she'd wake to find this had all been a dream, a vivid, heart-pumping, beautiful dream. But the long day joined forces with the slow caresses Ryan ran up and down her back to drag her toward oblivion. She went under, smiling all the way.

A DREAM. It was just a dream.

Ryan couldn't get enough air, no matter how hard he breathed. Sweat ran down his body in a thousand tributaries.

"Ryan?"

The voice, a female's, startled him and he spun toward it. It seemed to take forever for the truth to coalesce in his brain. Brooke. In his bed. Where they'd made love.

He wiped his hand over his face and tried to get the shaking under control.

"Ryan, what's wrong?"

"Nothing." He launched himself from the bed and strode into the bathroom, shutting the door behind him. He turned on the faucet and splashed his face with water, trying to wash away the remnants of the nightmare.

Why did he have to dream about that day tonight of

all nights? Why, damn it? He looked at his reflection and pushed down the need to punch the mirror. All that would accomplish would be messing up his one good hand just as the other one had almost healed.

He should go out and comfort Brooke, or maybe he should just ignore her and let her leave. Maybe now she and everyone else would see he was no good for anyone's future if he couldn't let go of the past, if he couldn't change it.

She knocked on the door. "Ryan, can I come in?"

He slammed a lid down on his self-pity party and opened the door. She stood there wrapped in a sheet, the moonlight shining in the window behind her making her look like an angel.

"I'm sorry," he said.

"For what?"

For dragging her into his life.

You didn't drag her, you fool. She walked into it willingly.

"For having a nightmare?" she asked.

He rubbed the back of his neck, wishing the right words would come to him. The way she was examining him made him squirm.

"I've been told I'm a pretty good listener," she said. "If you want to talk about it."

She could tell more was going on, and he didn't know how he felt about that. Part of him was touched that she could know him so well in so short a time. Part felt raw and exposed, the exact things he'd guarded against since coming home. Suddenly exhausted to the point he thought he might collapse, he walked past her and sank onto the side of the bed. Brooke didn't let the space between them stand and came to sit beside him.

"Like you told me, you don't have to say anything

if you don't want to. But I will listen, however long it takes."

He turned his head and looked her in the eyes, their color masked in the dimness of the room. But he could see them as clearly as if they stood in the middle of a sunny meadow. "It's ugly." Was he really considering telling her?

"Everyone's seen some type of ugly before."

"Not like this."

She touched his leg, skimming her palm over the scar that ran from the middle of his thigh to the base of his knee. Or what had once been his knee.

"Does it have anything to do with this?"

He stared at her hand caressing the constant reminder of what he'd done and almost pushed it away. He didn't want her tainted by what it represented. But he wasn't strong enough to relinquish the comfort that simple touch gave him. Whether he deserved it or not, he drank it in like a man dying of thirst.

He took a deep, painful breath and began to speak. "I was stationed in an Iraqi village about thirty miles outside Baghdad. It was a hotbed of insurgency, so we were always on the lookout for suspicious activity. One day, while we were patrolling the edge of a marketplace, I noticed someone heading toward the busiest area who was wearing a little too much clothing for how hot it was. I knew in my gut it was a suicide bomber and I called out for the person to stop. I couldn't even tell if it was a man or woman. Everything seemed to happen in slow motion and in the blink of an eye at the same time. I saw all those unsuspecting people in the same moment the bomber went for the detonator." His stomach churned at the vividness of the memory. The heat baking his head beneath his helmet. The sweat trickling down his back beneath his uniform. The sounds of Arabic being spoken, words he didn't understand. "I didn't hesitate. I shot her in the head, and the bomb didn't go off."

"Then it was a woman."

He swallowed hard, and it felt as if his throat was lined with knives. When he looked up at Brooke, he didn't know what he was looking for. Understanding? Absolution? Condemnation?

"It was a teenage girl. A fourteen-year-old girl."

Chapter Eleven

Brooke couldn't hide her shock, and she saw how it affected Ryan by how some sliver of hope died inside him. No, she would not be responsible for that. She grasped his hand before he could pull away.

"You didn't know."

"But she's just as dead."

"And a lot of other innocent people aren't because of what you did."

He laughed once, but it held not the tiniest drop of humor. "That's what everyone else says." He cursed. "They even gave me a damn medal. Said I'd saved not only Iraqi citizens but also American soldiers. As soon as I could walk again, I flushed it down the toilet."

"How were you hurt?"

He hesitated, as if he was mired in the horrible memory that had obviously chased him even in sleep. "After I shot the girl, saw her face staring up wide-eyed at the sky, people with guns came out of the woodwork. I was still in shock when the bullets and grenades started flying. It's a miracle none of them hit the bomb and set it off. But in the confusion, I got too close to one of the grenades. Damn near blew my leg off. They had to put a rod in my thigh and totally rebuilt my knee, mostly with mechanical parts."

"They must have done a good job because I've never noticed you limp."

"I've perfected the art of hiding it so I don't have to answer questions I'd rather avoid. Part of me wishes I could forget everything, but another part thinks I should have to live with the memory every day." He hung his head, shook it slowly back and forth. "She was just a kid."

She squeezed his hand harder, making sure he was paying attention. "And it's not your fault that someone filled her head with hate. As awful as it seems to say, you did the right thing. Think of all the mothers, fathers, husbands, wives, sons and daughters you saved."

"My brain knows that."

"But your heart still grieves the senseless loss."

"Yeah, I guess."

She cupped his jaw and forced him to look at her. "Listen to me. You are a good man. The simple fact that you torture yourself about that girl proves that to me. A lesser man wouldn't have cared, would have seen her as the enemy or just a casualty of war."

He stared at her so hard that she felt he was searching for her innermost soul.

"You make me want to believe that," he said.

"Good. Because it's true."

"How can you know that?"

"Call it gut instinct." And she was positive—had never been more positive about anything. But where had that gut instinct been when she'd met Chris? Had it taken going through the horrible months with him for it to be born?

"All those weeks I lay in that hospital bed, all I wanted to do was die." He shook his head. "I knew it didn't make sense. She'd been trying to kill people, her own people. But I couldn't get the look on her face out of my mind. It was shock. I could never figure out if it was shock that she'd failed or that she'd been talked into being a bomber in the first place."

"If you'd known she was a girl, would you have done anything differently?"

His mouth opened partially, but nothing came out. His forehead scrunched as if no one had ever asked him that question.

"She didn't give you a choice."

After several beats of silence, he finally spoke. "You're amazing."

"Because I tell the truth?" A pang of guilt squeezed her as she said those words because she wasn't telling him the full truth about herself, was she? She could tell herself all day that it was to protect herself, to protect him and his family, but it still felt wrong. But what choice did she have? Chris had power, and he wasn't afraid to use it.

"Because you don't treat me like I might break."

"Is that how everyone else treats you?"

"I'm not saying I haven't given them reason. The memories, they don't just show up in nightmares. I never know when they might hit."

"You've suffered post-traumatic stress?" She knew too much about that herself. All the evidence she needed was her little freakout in the dark the other night.

He nodded. "I've tried so hard to make it stop, so my family would stop worrying. Mom, especially. She thinks she hides it, but I can see it in her eyes sometimes."

"That's what moms do, they worry. It doesn't matter if you've been to war or fallen out of a tree and broken your wrist."

The edge of his mouth quirked a little. "You or your sister?"

"Both of us, actually."

He lifted his hand and ran his thumb over her lips. "I think you just might be my angel."

He kissed her again, and this time what stirred within her felt suspiciously like more than desire.

ONLY THE BAREST hint of a new day was filtering into Ryan's bedroom when Brooke woke the next morning. It had been a long time since she'd felt so cherished in a man's arms, so warm, so happy. In truth, she wasn't sure she'd ever experienced such a feeling. There was no stopping the smile that spread across her face. Not wanting to wake Ryan, she eased to a position where she could watch him sleep.

He looked so different from the night before, relaxed and at peace. She hoped the horrible dream that had haunted him for so long would leave him be.

She smiled at his mussed hair, a result of more enthusiastic lovemaking after they'd talked. She'd wanted to give him good memories to replace the bad. And, to be honest, she'd wanted to feel him again, experience that incredible pleasure he gave her.

As the light increased in the room, more of his features were visible, making it hard to resist running her fingers over them. But he deserved restful sleep not haunted by demons.

Brooke let more minutes tick by than she should, but finally she had to move. Before she could go to work, she had to sneak back to the bunkhouse for a shower and clean clothes. As she slid her legs over the side of the bed, Ryan roused, wrapped his arms around her waist and kissed her neck.

"Where do you think you're going?" He said it in a playful, sexy voice, not in the overbearing way Chris had developed toward the end of their relationship.

"I have to get ready for work."

"I have a shower. I could even help you." He nipped at her ear, sparking the beginnings of desire within her.

With her skin heating, she wriggled out of his grasp and stood, taking a sheet to wrap around her. "You are a bad influence."

"You're the one who led me to bed. Not that it wasn't an excellent idea." He waggled his eyebrows and smiled.

She pointed at him. "Ryan Teague, you are more like Simon than you'd ever admit."

"Are you saying I have a way with the ladies?" He scooted closer to the edge of the bed.

"I'm saying you are an incredible flirt hidden in shy guy clothing."

"Last I checked, I wasn't wearing clothing."

"See, that's what I'm talking about."

He grabbed at her sheet, grasping it before she could move out of reach. "And I believe I know someone else who isn't wearing anything beneath that sheet."

She squealed and laughed as he tugged her into his arms and swung her back onto the bed, covering her with that big, wonderful body of his. Though she could go on kissing him all day, she had to break away. She pressed her hands against his naked chest and almost lost her willpower.

"Ryan, I have to get to work."

"Will you come back later?"

His request touched her heart. "If you want me to."

He captured her mouth in a mind-melting kiss. "Does that answer your question?"

Indeed, it did.

BROOKE MANAGED TO slip past the main house without seeing anyone. Only when she closed the bunkhouse door behind her did she breathe easier. Only then did she allow herself a full smile and a squeal of excitement that made her feel like a teenager again. Was this the reason she'd been attracted to the ad for Vista Hills? Was fate offering up something wonderful because she'd already had her share of not so wonderful?

Unfortunately, she had no time to simply sit and relive the previous night. She rushed through her shower, trying not to imagine Ryan under the flow of water with her. After pulling on clothes as she rushed for the door, she ran until she was in view of the main house then slowed to a normal pace.

Maybe thanks to the party the night before, she had the kitchen to herself when she arrived. It gave her time to slow her heartbeat and breathing, to try to shove the memory of Ryan's hands on her body away from the front of her mind.

"Good morning."

Brooke jumped at the sound of Merline's voice and dropped the knife she'd been about to use to cut up some apples.

"Sorry, I didn't mean to startle you." Merline strolled into the room, and Brooke would swear there was a knowing twinkle in her eyes. "You seemed a million miles away."

Not near that far.

"Just still sleepy." Oh, no, would Merline immediately determine the reason for her lack of sleep? "It was a long day yesterday." Good grief, everything she said made her feel as though she was proclaiming, "I had sex with your son, several times. And I liked it!" She needed to just shut up.

"You looked like you were having fun last night."

"Yeah," she said as she picked up the knife and placed it in the sink. "Hard not to be happy at a wedding."

"Can't say I remember the last time I've seen Ryan dance."

Brooke made a noncommittal sound and grabbed a clean knife from the butcher block. A few moments passed, the only sound that of the knife slicing through crisp Granny Smith apples.

"You did a marvelous job yesterday," Merline said, blissfully changing the subject.

"Thank you."

Merline held up a piece of paper, waving it in the air. "And I'm impressed by this list of ideas you came up with for adding guest activities. I particularly like the one for educational classes on the history of the area. I have a friend at the local museum who will jump on that." She consulted the list. "Flora and fauna, wine tastings, crafts classes. All wonderful." She placed the paper on the island and tapped it with her finger. "You have a real talent for this."

Brooke made the mistake of meeting Merline's gaze. There she saw knowledge, not of what Brooke had done the night before but that she was more than what she said.

"I'm just a cook."

"No, you're not." Brooke froze as Merline continued. "I'd like to offer you a bit more responsibility and the title of guest services coordinator."

Brooke's head spun. Everything was happening too fast. Though she didn't feel, deep down, that she'd made a mistake with Ryan, she wondered if she was letting her emotions get in the way of logic and clarity.

"I don't know what to say."

"Just take time to think about it. I'm off to the gallery for a while. After lunch, take the rest of the afternoon off."

Brooke couldn't help the feeling that she was getting special treatment. "That isn't necessary."

"I'm sure you can find something to do." With another of those smiles that said Merline possessed an uncanny ability to see beyond the surface, she gave a little wave and headed out the back door.

Thing was, Merline was right. She could think of a lot of ways to spend a free afternoon, and they all involved one sexy Texan.

RYAN CAUGHT HIMSELF whistling and stopped in the middle of carving an edge of an angel wing. When was the last time he'd whistled? He couldn't remember. He also couldn't remember the last time he'd felt so alive. Sure, the memory of that Iraqi girl was still there, always would be. But it was somehow different, as if the scene had been cast in a different light, one more forgiving.

He looked down at the angel, rubbed away wood shavings. She was different from all the others, too, kinder, gentler. Because of Brooke.

When he thought about how different he felt inside now compared to the same time yesterday, it didn't seem possible. He kept fearing the lightness in his chest would go away, allowing all the dark, heavy guilt to gather there again. He'd carried that guilt for so long, he'd nearly forgotten what it was like to exist without it. He still couldn't figure out why Brooke's words had made him look at the girl's death differently when no one else's had ever made a dent.

But he was glad they had. Because for the first time since that horrible day, he felt as if he truly had something to look forward to.

He glanced at the clock, realizing only three minutes had ticked by since the last time he'd looked. Was this what Nathan had gone through when he'd realized he felt more for Grace, beyond that they shared a child?

The phone rang, pulling him from his mental meanderings.

"Vista Hills Furniture."

"Ryan Teague?"

"Yes."

"This is Libby Prentiss from *Uniquely Texas*. I'd like to talk to you about doing a program on your furniture."

Ten minutes later, he'd scheduled an interview with the TV program that focused on, well, things that were unique to Texas. His mom might pass out when she learned he'd agreed to it, but he guessed he had Brooke to thank for that, too. It was as though he'd only been existing for the past two years, and now he really wanted to live. Just as Simon had challenged him to do.

Lunchtime came and went, and even if some of the guests had lingered, he began to wonder if he'd been wrong about Brooke, that she wouldn't keep her promise and come back to see him. He was two steps out the door, heading to his parents' house, when he stopped himself.

This wasn't him, not even the person he'd been before he'd covered himself in camo and flown off to the Middle East. He returned to his shop and started working on an armoire. As he sanded the wood, he tried not to overanalyze everything that had happened in the past twenty-fours hours. Damn, guys didn't do that kind of stuff.

"Hey." Brooke's voice drew his attention to the other end of the shop.

"Hey." She'd come back. And that made him ridiculously happy. He stood and crossed to her, pulling her into his arms. "Miss me?"

She looked up at him with a confused look on her face. "Who are you again?"

He showed her with his mouth, and she responded not as a stranger but as someone who knew him very well. "Remember me now?" he asked when they broke the kiss.

"It's coming back to me." She ran her fingers through his hair. "You greet all your visitors like that?"

"Sure. Why do you think I sell so much furniture?"

She swatted at his chest, but he just laughed and kissed her again.

"So, how much time do you have before you have to go back to work?"

"As it happens, your mom gave me the afternoon off."

He leaned his head against hers. "She knows."

"Yes, I think so."

He pulled back and captured her gaze. "Well, good."

She seemed startled by his response, and honestly he was, too. But he didn't want to hide anymore.

"Is that okay with you?" he asked.

She didn't speak, just nodded, but that was enough. She lowered her eyes, scanning the room.

"You carved another angel." She stepped out of his embrace and walked over to the workbench. Her touch seemed reverent as she picked up the angel and traced its features with her fingertip.

"But this one is different," he said.

"How so?"

"I'll show you." He nodded toward the house then headed inside. He heard her follow as he walked toward his bedroom. He didn't expect the nervous energy that started to churn in his stomach. No one had ever seen the angels, not even the therapist who'd urged him to find some form of expression for all his bottled-up feelings.

He went straight to the tall corner cabinet in his room, the one he'd built when it hadn't felt right to keep the angels tossed in a box. With a deep breath, he opened it then stepped out of the way.

Brooke stared, her mouth partially open, her eyes taking in the details of the dozens of angels sitting on the shelves. Still without speaking, she walked to the cabinet and examined the carvings more closely.

"Ryan, these are beautiful. But heartbreaking in a way." She looked down at the angel in her hand, the one she'd carried in from the workshop. "But not this one. She seems…full of joy."

"That wasn't intentional. It just happened." He relived the jolt of surprise that had rocketed through him when he'd realized his carving tools were not doing what they normally did when he lost himself in one of the angel carvings. Instead of closed or sad eyes, the new angel's were inexplicably full of light. Her wings didn't seem weighed down but rather lifted to their full width. Her hands were extended, palms up, one of them filled with a dove.

He came to stand behind Brooke and reached past her into the cabinet to grab one of the angels. "This is the first one I carved. I'd only been home a week, and my mind felt as destroyed as my knee."

The angel was crude in design, obviously the work of a beginner. He was afraid to look at it too long, scared he'd feel the twisting anguish he'd been trying to get rid of by carving it.

"Did it help?"

He placed the angel back on the shelf. "I honestly don't remember, but I know whenever things got really bad or I couldn't sleep for nightmares, I'd end up with a chunk of wood in one hand and a carving knife in the other. I can't say I was even thinking about what I was doing." He motioned toward the shelves of angels looking back at them. "But one of these always seemed to appear in my hands."

"Guardian angels."

He shrugged. He'd never examined the why too closely, just knew that something about carving them calmed him, kept him from losing his mind.

He watched as Brooke examined the entire collection, more than fifty angels.

"You can see how you changed over time."

"Really?"

She pulled out one of his early, clunkier attempts. "See how she seems to curl in on herself, how she's looking down. You were likely feeling the same way." She pointed to another, made about a year ago. "She's standing straighter, but still not looking forward." Brooke lifted the new angel. "You've let her go."

And he knew the "her" wasn't the angel. It was that Iraqi girl staring sightless up at the wide, blue sky.

Chapter Twelve

The raw emotion, the pain and eventual healing flowing out of the carved angels touched Brooke so deeply it was difficult not to cry. That Ryan was sharing it with her—when some deep instinct told her he'd never done that with anyone—meant so much. She couldn't even fully describe the well of warmth and appreciation filling her heart.

There was something else building in her heart, too, but she was scared to give it a name.

Ryan touched the angel in her hand, the one he'd been working on when she'd arrived. "I want you to have this." He paused. "I don't think I would have ever carved it without you."

She shook her head. "I've done so little. Your family, they've been here all along."

"They have. But…" He was quiet so long that she didn't think he was going to finish voicing his thought. Maybe he didn't know how. "I don't pretend to understand it, but you've changed me. Made me remember who I used to be, who I want to be again."

So much truth, coming from a man of normally few words, really meant something. And Brooke felt them echo inside her, as if she'd spoken those words to him. She turned and cupped his jaw.

"I know what you mean."

Ryan lifted his unbandaged hand and tilted her face up. After staring deep into her eyes for what felt like long minutes but was only mere seconds, he lowered his mouth to hers in the sweetest kiss. The tenderness made that unnamed emotion in her chest flirt with a name—love.

As improbable as it would no doubt seem to outsiders looking in, she was falling in love with Ryan Teague.

She expected the kiss to lead to the bed, but Ryan broke contact and led her toward the door instead.

"Where are you taking me now?"

"Someplace you're going to like."

Truer words had never been spoken. An hour after he'd led her to the barn and saddled a horse, they'd climbed up one of the ranch's trails to a ridge that overlooked Blue Falls and the lake. It shimmered like a diamond in the distance.

"Oh, Ryan. It's gorgeous." It felt as close to heaven as she'd ever been. Up here, the breeze was cooler, caressing her warm cheeks.

"I knew you'd like it. It's the highest point on the ranch, highest point for miles around." He sat on the edge of the cliff and motioned for her to sit in front of him. Ryan held her hand firmly as she stepped between his legs and sat so that her own legs dangled over the edge of the rock.

"It feels like a different world up here," she said.

"I remember the first time I was able to walk up here following my injury. It took me all day, and I've never been so tired in my life. I scared Mom to death because I didn't get back until like ten at night."

"But you felt better for doing it, didn't you?"

He wrapped his arms more tightly around her and spoke close to her ear. "Yeah."

She listened to the breeze ruffling the trees below them. "This place really is amazing. I know you've been through a lot, but I also think you're a lucky man. To have this kind of connection to the land, being surrounded by such a tight-knit family. It's sort of the iconic American dream."

Ryan entwined the fingers of his uninjured hand with hers. "There are other reasons I feel lucky, too."

She smiled without looking back at him.

"I hope you're feeling at home here," he said.

"I am." She was constantly surprised by how much so.

"Good."

Again, silence stretched between them, but it wasn't uncomfortable. If anything, it encouraged the knots still hiding inside Brooke to ease. She scanned the horizon, thinking how incredibly different it was from what she was used to seeing in the city, even from the mountains of West Virginia. There was something wonderfully open and freeing in being able to see so far. No more feeling trapped.

"What are you thinking?" he asked.

"Sometimes it scares me how much I like it here."

"Why?"

She shrugged, unwilling to share all the thoughts that were really running through her head. That getting so attached to a place and the people there wasn't wise when it all still had a tinge of temporary clinging to it.

Ryan kissed her temple. "I'll try not to give you a reason to leave here."

She closed her eyes and tried not to think about how Ryan wouldn't be the one to cause her to flee. If anything, she'd leave to protect him and his family. He'd gone through too much already and shouldn't have to deal with her mess.

"How did you pick here to relocate?" he asked.

"It sounds crazy, but I saw an ad for the position when I was doing random job searches online. I just had this overwhelming feeling this was where I had to go. My sister thought I'd lost my mind."

He was quiet for several endless seconds, and she feared she'd said too much. Had invited questions she didn't feel she could answer.

"This seems to be a good place for starting over," he finally said.

She took a deep, slow breath then let it out as she watched a bird drift on the air. Free as a bird. That's how she felt now, and she felt like laughing and crying at the same time at the realization.

"Yeah, it does."

BROOKE HOWLED WITH laughter along with everyone else at Simon's attempt at pin the tail on the donkey. He wasn't even in the ballpark.

"Uncle Simon, that's a lamp!" Evan said.

Simon spun toward the boy. "Maybe you need a tail."

Evan squealed and scrambled over the back of the couch. Ryan picked him up and swung him onto his shoulders. That increasingly familiar emotion moved in her chest again, causing her to smile in his direction. His gaze locked with hers and he smiled back.

It'd been a week since their ride up to the top of the ranch, and they'd spent almost all of their spare time together. Sometimes helping each other work, sometimes going for walks. And there was plenty of time spent in bed, too. With each passing day, she marveled at her remarkable good fortune and wondered more and more how she could have ever fancied herself in love with Chris. Because though neither she nor Ryan had said those words, it was clear that was the path they were heading down. When she saw him, it was literally impossible not to smile.

Guilt still stabbed her that she wasn't being honest with him, but she was so wrapped up in the lie now it was hard to see a way out. She'd like to say she kept mum about her past strictly to protect herself, Ryan and his family, but that wasn't the full truth either. Now that her heart was involved, she was afraid revealing the truth would cause her to lose him.

Nathan finally snatched the donkey tail away from Simon, saying he was a danger to public safety, and they all settled in to watch Merline open her birthday presents. Merline oohed and aahed at each one, but she looked on the verge of tears when she opened the one from Ryan and read the note. Brooke had convinced him to save the birdhouse for another occasion and to make an angel for his mother. After all, it was Merline who'd really been the one to stand beside him as he recovered.

Though the room was full of people and tonight she felt more a part of this family than she could have ever thought imaginable, watching this moment seemed too private and she edged her way into the kitchen. If anyone asked, she'd use the excuse of wanting a second slice of cake.

When she heard footsteps, at first she thought it was Ryan but realized quickly that the sound wasn't right. As she turned away from the island, Merline took both of Brooke's hands in hers. "I want to thank you for giving me the best birthday present I've ever received."

What? Sure, the blown-glass flower arrangement was nice, but it was nothing compared to the carved angel.

For a brief moment, Merline bit her bottom lip. "You gave me my son back."

Brooke didn't know what to say. In the silence stretching between them, Merline wrapped Brooke in a hug. A lump formed in Brooke's throat because the contact made her miss her own mother even more. With a smile and a pat on Brooke's cheek, Merline returned to the party.

Needing some time alone to push back tears, she stepped outside. As soon as she crossed from the light of the kitchen to the dark night outside, her cell phone rang. She jumped at the unexpected sound. The only person not in the house behind her who had this number was her sister.

With her heart beating fast, she answered. "Hello?"

"Brooke, it's Holly."

Brooke heard a slight tremor in her sister's voice, but she didn't immediately ask why it was present. She didn't want to hear anything that might be the equivalent of another bomb going off in her life. "How are you all?"

"Good, just working, you know. Caitlyn won the school spelling bee for the second grade."

"That's wonderful. Give her a hug and kiss from me."

"I will."

Brooke could tell Holly wasn't fully invested in the chitchat part of the conversation, so she took a deep breath and asked the question hanging between them. "What is it?"

"Chris showed up at my office today."

"What?" Brooke's heart started beating so fast it reverberated against her eardrums. "He didn't hurt you, did he? Threaten you?"

"No, but I got the distinct feeling that he knew that I know where you are. He had someone with him, a guy who walked around the office while Chris talked to me. I don't know what he was doing."

"I'm so sorry. I never meant for this to touch you in any way." Tears pooled in her eyes and each word was more difficult to say than the last. "I..." She couldn't believe what she was thinking, what she was about to say, but she'd do anything to keep her sister and nieces—the only family she had left—safe. "I'll go back to D.C."

Holly cut her off before she could say anything else. "You'll do no such thing. You've given up too much already just because he's crazy."

"But I can't live with it if anything happens—"

"Nothing will happen to us. I'm more worried about you. I know we've been careful about communications, but you said he's powerful, knows powerful people. What if he figures out how to track you there?"

"I've been very careful." She wouldn't let her sister know she feared the same thing. Instead of a lobbyist trying to encourage votes on Capitol Hill, it sometimes seemed as if Chris was CIA or something. He had ways of finding things out.

"I wish he'd just let go, move on," Holly said.

"He will, eventually." Brooke wasn't so sure, but it was her most fervent hope.

In the background, she heard a door close.

"The girls just came in from playing. They'll want to talk to you if I don't get off here."

"No, let me talk to them." She needed that connection with their innocence and sweetness, to hear for herself that they were okay.

There was some shuffling of the phone, then Emma's little voice came on. "Hi, Aunt Brooke."

"Hey there, punkin. How are you?"

"Good. When are you coming to visit?"

Brooke pressed her eyes closed and swallowed hard. "I'm not sure, sweetie. I'm getting settled in a new job."

"Oh."

After some chatter about Emma's new guinea pig, Princess, the phone was passed to Caitlyn.

"Hey, I hear you won your spelling bee," Brooke said.

"Yeah. I beat out Jason Trainer. He thinks he's smarter than everyone else."

Brooke laughed. "Well, he's not the best speller, is he?"

"Nope."

Brooke smiled at the pride in her niece's voice. How she missed those girls. She hadn't seen them terribly often when she was in D.C., but Texas seemed a world away. As though they might suddenly grow up and she would miss it all.

Once the girls relinquished the phone to their mother, Holly asked, "How are things going there? Are you still liking it?"

"Yes, it's great. The Teagues are wonderful people. I think Mom and Dad would have liked them."

"I'm glad. Maybe when everything settles, we can come visit."

"I'd like that." When everything settled. She tried not to think about how Chris might never give up his obsession, how she might have to live a lie for the rest of her life. Her heart hurt at the thought of keeping something as important as who she really was from Ryan, but what choice did she have? If she lived openly under her own name, that would just make it easier for Chris to find her.

A chill ran down her back as she remembered the words he'd spoken when she'd tried to leave before. "You will never leave." It hadn't been so much the words as how he'd said them, the look in his eyes. He hadn't explained the consequences of her leaving, but he hadn't needed to. His tone and expression told her everything. If she tried, she'd live to regret it. She'd allowed those words to control her for far too long, until she couldn't stand it anymore. She'd finally decided the risk was worth it. But she wasn't about to risk her family.

"Holly, promise me something."

"Okay." Her sister sounded hesitant, as if she knew she wasn't going to like what Brooke was about to say.

"If he contacts you again, let me know immediately." Even knowing the inevitable result, to protect her family she'd go back to him, try to figure out another way of making a break so that he left them all alone.

"Brooke?"

She jumped at the sound of Ryan's voice at the back door.

"Who's that?" Holly asked in her ear.

She held up an index finger to Ryan. "It's my boss's son," she said low to into the phone.

"You're still working this late?"

"We're having a birthday party for his mom."

"That sounds nice. Just what you need."

"Yeah, I gotta go. But promise me, okay?"

Holly hesitated but eventually made the promise that allowed Brooke to breathe a little easier. "Thanks. I love you."

"I love you, too. Be careful. And enjoy your new start, okay?"

Brooke glanced back at Ryan. "I am."

She ended the call just as Ryan stepped close to her. "Everything okay?"

She pasted on a smile. "Yeah. That was my sister. I didn't mean to be rude and disappear, but it was easier to hear out here." Even that small lie caused an unwelcome twinge, smacked her with the fact she was building a relationship on lies.

He looked down at her as if searching her face for something she was hiding. His hand found its way to hers. The warmth and strength of his helped steady her.

"We should go back inside," she said and started to step toward the door.

"I have a better idea." He pulled her close and kissed her.

When the kiss ended, she whispered against his lips. "That *was* a good idea."

After another kiss, Ryan allowed her to lead him back inside. But she went no farther than the kitchen as Ryan continued on into the living room, where his family was still having a good time if the laughter was any indication. She braced herself against the island and scanned the faces. Little Evan who was always a ball of energy and desperate to emulate every action of his father, grandfather and uncles. Merline, who had effortlessly filled the hole Brooke's mother's death had left. Simon, who was a flirt, yes, but also someone who could make her laugh. Grace, who looked at her new husband with so much love, it was inspiring. Nathan, who watched Grace much the same way.

And Ryan. Brooke's heart felt as if it expanded as she looked at him. He'd come to mean so much to her in so little time. And the true miracle was that he seemed to feel the same way about her, but without any demands or hint of being overbearing. He was the kind of man she should have loved all along.

She did love him. There was nothing else she was more sure of. But even that wasn't enough to keep her here if Chris threatened her family. Or Ryan's. The realization that the Teagues had become like a second family to her made the mere idea of leaving this place heartbreaking.

Ryan looked up and met her gaze, giving her a private smile. She smiled back and hoped the number of smiles between them weren't numbered.

Chapter Thirteen

As the interview with *Uniquely Texas* progressed, Ryan kept glancing toward the door to his shop, hoping that Brooke would appear. After all, she was part of his story, helping him when he was injured and encouraging him to bring his angels to light. Just the night before, as they'd lain together in his bed, he'd made the decision to do exactly that. The ones he'd made with that Iraqi girl in mind would forever stay private, but something had changed in him in the past few days. He'd gotten ideas for innumerable angel designs, had started on a couple of them. He wanted to surprise Brooke by revealing that she was the inspiration.

But as the interview drew to a close, he realized she wasn't going to show. And that didn't sit well with him. The story didn't seem complete without her.

"I'd like to give you all a quick tour of the guest ranch operation, if I could."

Libby Prentiss, the host of the show, glanced at the time. "We could probably spare a few minutes, just shoot a little bit for background."

It was enough to get them to the main house, where Brooke was no doubt busy in the kitchen.

He showed them the barn, pointed out where his dad and Nathan were giving riding lessons, even shared a bit of the ranch's long history. When they reached the house, he spotted Brooke right where he'd pictured her, at the island preparing lunch for the guests. His mom sat across from her, consulting some paperwork. Wonderful, he could introduce the two most important women in his life.

As he pulled the door open and ushered the crew inside, he caught movement out of the corner of his eye.

Brooke had spotted the camera and stepped away from the island. Her eyes widened ,though he got the added feeling that she was trying to hide it.

"Excuse me," she said. "I have to make a phone call."

He rounded the island and spoke low to her. "Brooke, I'd like you to be a part of the TV piece."

She waved off the idea. "I'm not much for cameras. Your mom will do a great job. Maybe she can mention the gallery, too." With a smile he'd swear was forced, she left the room and closed herself in his mother's office.

When he turned back around, his mom looked as surprised as he felt but she covered it well.

Not wanting the crew to sense anything off, he said, "Looks like our cook is a little camera shy. But this is my mother, Merline Teague, the heart and soul of Vista Hills."

She gestured to deflect his praise, and he could tell that endeared her to Libby. The reporter launched right into her questions about the ranch's guest operations.

He only half listened as Libby and his mother talked about the day-to-day operations and new offerings on the horizon. Most of his attention, however, had shifted from the interview to Brooke's reaction. He hadn't meant to make her uncomfortable and couldn't help but wonder if this had something to do with her old life. Was it more than some sort of bad breakup?

The crew wrapped up shooting footage and departed, leaving his mother and him perplexed in the kitchen.

"Some people have a phobia of cameras," his mom said.

"Yeah, I guess." Instinct was telling him it was more than that. Had whoever she'd been with before convinced her she wasn't attractive? Was that why she didn't like cameras?

"I'm heading into town for a while," his mom said with a glance toward her home office.

Thankful for the opportunity to talk to Brooke alone, he headed toward the closed door then knocked. "Can I come in?" She didn't answer, so he cracked the door enough to poke his head inside. Brooke looked up from where she was writing something. "They're gone."

The tenseness in her shoulders and the tight expression on her face relaxed visibly as she lowered her gaze.

He opened the door the rest of the way and stood propped against the doorframe. "Why the disappearing act?"

She looked down at the paper on the desk. "I told you."

"This have anything to do with a guy you left behind?"

"Why would you say that?"

He noticed she didn't meet his eyes, just kept writing on the notepad in front of her.

"I feel like there's something you're not telling me."

It took her too long to answer, enough time for his stomach to knot.

"I was interviewed on TV once, in high school, and

I totally flubbed it up. It was like I couldn't even speak English. It was mortifying."

Relief poured through Ryan at the ring of truth in her answer. He felt bad for doubting her.

"Sorry for springing the camera crew on you."

"It's okay." She smiled. "At least I didn't run screaming from the house." Her words were a touch shaky, revealing just how much the near-miss with the camera had bothered her.

Brooke stood and rounded the desk, taking the paper with her. "I better finish preparing lunch. Looks like everyone is working up an appetite out there." She motioned in the general direction of the corral outside the barn.

He reached for her hand, took it gently in his own. "I'll come by after lunch is over. We can do something this afternoon."

She smiled. "You'd better be making furniture because I predict you're going to be getting a lot of new orders soon." She held up the paper in her hand. "Plus, I need to do some grocery shopping."

"Okay, tonight then."

She nodded and made a noise that barely sounded like agreement. His heart lurched at her tone, as if she was pulling away. But why? Surely surprising her with a TV camera wasn't enough to cause that.

He smiled back, telling himself he was just looking for problems where none existed.

Now if he could only convince himself of that.

BROOKE HAD THOUGHT about feigning a headache to have the night alone to think, but all the worrying that had plagued her throughout the afternoon turned the headache into reality. Merline had even sent her home early to get some rest. But despite taking some ibuprofen and slipping into her most comfortable pajamas, she couldn't rest. Couch, bed, chair—it didn't matter where she tried, nothing worked.

Finally, she slipped into a T-shirt, a pair of shorts and sneakers and stood facing the front door. She wanted so much to go see Ryan, to have him wrap her in his arms and tell her everything was going to be fine.

But that wasn't reality, was it? Reality was the fact that she was too scared to unbolt the door in front of her, let alone traipse to Ryan's in the dark of night. She retraced her steps and collapsed into an armchair. It was best if she stayed away from Ryan as much as she could. If she couldn't even tell him the truth, why was she trying to fool herself that they had a chance at a happily-ever-after? Besides, instinct was yelling at her that her short reprieve might come to an end, and that before it did she needed to figure out her next step.

No matter how long she sat and considered where she might go next, nothing felt right. Not like it had when she'd seen the ad for Vista Hills.

Unable to think about going anywhere else any longer, she curled up in a ball and did her best to turn off her mind. She lost track of the minutes and hours, but eventually sleep won and pulled her under. Her last conscious thought was that she hoped sleep would bring her some peace, and some answers.

EVERY DAY IT BECAME harder and harder to manufacture excuses for not spending time with Ryan. She'd used the grocery trip already, and going into town to buy Caitlyn a birthday present, the extra work necessary for a day-long teachers' retreat the ranch was hosting. She'd allowed Ryan to get her alone for quick kisses in the kitchen or outside the back door, but she wouldn't go to his place or allow him to come to hers. She couldn't get more attached, couldn't let him do the same.

By the time she'd managed four days of dodging, she was exhausted, her nerves frayed. She'd even considered packing up and leaving in the middle of the night to remove herself from temptation, but that smacked too much of when she'd fled Chris. The Teagues—Ryan—were not the same as Chris. She wouldn't treat them the same way.

As she pulled a sheet of sugar cookies from the oven, Simon wandered into the kitchen and snatched one of them, juggling it to cool it. Forgetting that she was trying to keep her distance, she swatted at him.

"Stop thieving my hard work."

He responded by snatching another.

"You're impossible," she said.

"Say, after you're done with the dinner crowd tonight, you should come out to the music hall. We're playing."

He had no idea how much she wanted to say yes. The thought of dancing in Ryan's arms again, like she had the first night they'd made love, wrapped her in a warmth she'd not felt in several days. But she had to stick to her plan of being friendly but distant.

"Sounds like fun, but I need to do some work tonight on some of the projects your mom and I have been talking about."

"They'll wait until tomorrow."

She turned her back to finish scooping the cookies off the sheet. Damn, he was persistent, and she was running out of excuses.

"Maybe next time."

"What's going on, Brooke? One minute, you and

Ryan are lovey-dovey, and the next you're keeping him at arm's length."

"I'm just trying to do my job."

"Bull. You're jerking him around, and he doesn't deserve that. He's been through enough."

"Simon, stop." Merline had come out of her office, and Brooke felt like running out the back door and not stopping until she got to California.

"It's true, Mom. This is the first time he's really acted normal since he got back, and she's ruining it."

"I said that's enough." This time Merline's voice was stronger, more like a mother disciplining a child. "Go to work."

Brooke sensed his hesitation, but he finally complied. But his accusations rang in her ears like a big, clanging cowbell. And they were all true. Unable to hold everything in any longer, fat tears leaked out and streamed down her cheeks. She dropped the spatula and swiped at the tears.

"Honey, what's wrong?"

"He's right, I'm ruining everything. I left to try to make things better, but it just keeps chasing me."

Merline stepped closer and took Brooke's hands in hers. "What's chasing you?"

Brooke met Merline's gaze through her wet lashes. "My past." She broke contact and paced across the kitchen, putting distance between herself and Merline. "Someone in my past."

Merline remained silent, giving Brooke the time she needed to tell her story. Part of Brooke was whispering that she should have shared this with Ryan if she truly cared about him, but the thought made her ill. She hated the idea of how he might look at her, like the victim she'd allowed herself to be.

"I dated someone, and for a while he seemed… perfect. Chris was good-looking, a successful lobbyist in Washington, interested in me. At least that's how he made it seem. Everything changed so gradually that I didn't realize it at first. And when I did, it was too late."

"Did he hit you?" Merline asked. Her question sounded like that of a protective mama bear, and it made fresh tears well in Brooke's eyes.

Brooke shook her head. "No. But the unspoken threat was there if I didn't do what he wanted." She sighed, wishing she could erase that part of her life that had ever been touched by Chris. "This is so embarrassing. It makes me feel like an idiot."

"You're not an idiot." Merline said it with such conviction that it gave Brooke the strength to go on.

"Looking back, I guess the first signs were when he'd be upset when I had to work late or when I went out with friends. I chalked it up to him just wanting to spend time with me. But then he started calling me more and more, like he was checking to see that I was where I was supposed to be. And he'd be at my place when I got home from work. It got to where I never had any time alone. The smothering was one thing, but…" She choked on the memory of what came next. "When I told him that I wanted to break up, that's when he got really scary. He said that he wouldn't let me go, that I didn't really want that either. He started spending the night every night, and I was afraid to say no."

She blinked against her tears.

"How did you get away?"

"It went on for a year, and I became the perfect actress. And then I did the thing he feared most. I ran away. I went to work like I normally did because I knew he made sure that's where I went before he went to work, and then I returned home. I packed only what I could in my car and left everything else behind, with no forwarding address. I went somewhere I had no connections and sold my car, went somewhere else to buy the one I have now. I paid cash I got from closing my checking account so he couldn't trace it."

"And that's why you came here? To hide?"

Brooke swiped at a tear that escaped as she nodded. If she'd ever thought it might be easier to tell Merline than it would have been Ryan, she'd been wrong. In some ways, it was worse because this was the woman she'd convinced to hire her under false pretenses. The one she now thought of as a mother figure.

Brooke's voice broke as she met Merline's too kind, too understanding eyes. She didn't deserve that kindness or understanding. "I lied to you. I didn't even tell you who I really am. My name isn't Brooke Vincent. It's Brooke Alder."

Movement out of the corner of her eye caught Brooke's attention. When she turned, her heart faltered. Sometime during her pacing confession, Ryan had come into the house. How much had he heard? She braced for a tirade of anger, but it didn't come. Instead, his face reflected pain. He turned and retraced his steps out the front door.

Feeling as though her life was crumbling around her, she hurried after him, catching him on the front porch.

"Ryan, wait." She didn't even try to mask the desperation in her voice. "I'm sorry."

"For which part? Lying to us? Or pretending to care about us?" He said "us" but she knew he meant him.

"I didn't plan this, caring about you."

"Good to know."

She couldn't stand how he looked at her, as if he'd

made a mistake in caring about her. He couldn't be that cruel, could he?

"How much did you hear?"

"Enough."

"How much, Ryan?"

"That you came here under a false name and that you're running away from something." He shook his head. "Did you break the law?"

She swallowed, hurt that he could think that. But she had no right to be hurt. She was the one at fault. Though she was still raw from confessing all to Merline, she repeated everything. She didn't let herself hope for forgiveness, not even when she saw how his expression and stiff stance changed to reflect some sympathy as she revealed more and more.

When she finished, he lifted his hand as if he might touch her, then let it drop back to his side. "I'm not him. I wouldn't have hurt you like that."

She ignored how his last sentence was in past tense, as if she'd blown her one and only chance with him.

"I know that now." She bit her lip to still the trembling there before going on. "I really do care about you, Ryan."

It would be so much easier to leave if she hadn't confessed that, but she couldn't help it. The past few days had been horrible, knowing he was so close and trying to be with her while she deliberately stayed away.

"Just not enough to be honest with me." He sounded more sad than angry, and she didn't know which hurt her more.

"I…" God, how did she make this better? "I wanted it to just go away, to protect you."

"I don't need protecting. I wish people would stop thinking I do."

She bit her trembling lip again as tears gathered in her eyes. "You don't understand. Chris is powerful, a big-time lobbyist in Washington. He knows people in high places, and he could find me if I didn't do something drastic."

He met her eyes, holding her gaze. "Is my family in danger?"

"No." But a *yes* echoed in her head.

"I need to be sure of that, Brooke."

"I've taken every precaution I could think of, but I'll leave if you want." It ripped her apart inside to even consider it.

"I didn't say that." He looked away, toward the pasture. "I'm upset, but I want you to be safe."

For a moment, she thought he might turn and pull her into his arms, might forgive her. Instead, he turned and descended the front steps.

She reached for him, but all she caught was air. "Ryan?"

"I need to be alone to think." Without looking at her, he started walking toward his home.

She drew her hand back and hugged it to her chest. More tears flowed down the same tracks along her cheeks, but these were worse. They burned as they escaped, and her heart felt as if a demon was inside her chest ripping chunks out of it and discarding them like unnecessary trash.

The front door opened, and suddenly Merline's arm was around her. Brooke didn't deserve the comfort, but she accepted it nonetheless. The way she was shaking, she might collapse into a heap of despair on the porch if she didn't.

"I'm so sorry. I didn't mean to hurt anyone."

"Shh," Merline said as she rubbed Brooke's arm and

hugged her tighter to her side. "Don't you worry. We won't let anyone hurt you."

Brooke pulled away. "No, I can't let you all become involved in this. He's already shown up at my sister's office in West Virginia. I've got to find a way to make sure he doesn't hurt anyone I care about just to get to me."

Merline braced her hands on her hips. "Don't you go getting any foolish ideas about falling on your sword or something. In case you hadn't noticed, we take care of our own here."

"But—"

"No buts. We've got enough big, tough Texans here that that city boy won't know what hit him. I even have an in with the sheriff," Merline said with a small smile.

"I'm not sure he'd agree with you."

"Never mind Simon. He's just watching out for his brother." Brooke glanced down the driveway, but Ryan had already disappeared.

"And give Ryan time," Merline said with a gentleness that made Brooke's breaking heart ache even more. "I've seen how he looks at you. He'll come around."

Brooke didn't know how Merline could think that.

But Merline hadn't seen the look of betrayal in Ryan's eyes just before he'd turned his back to Brooke. Before he'd walked away for what might be the last time.

RYAN WONDERED WHAT he should call his other half because since he'd walked away from Brooke the day before he'd felt a little like Jekyll and Hyde. Half of him wished he'd never met Brooke, wanted her to pack up and leave, taking her issues with her. But half of him realized that was hurt talking, and he wanted to go wrap her in his protective arms, to make sure this Chris guy never got anywhere near her again.

Unable to sleep in the bed where he'd made love to her, he'd spent the night in the shop working before collapsing on the couch for a few hours of less-than-restful sleep. Now fortified with some industrial-strength coffee, he was at it again. He'd knocked out two complete orders overnight, but now he felt as if he was trying to work with ten thumbs instead of his normal arrangement of fingers.

He cursed and paced a circle around the shop. Unable to stand its confines anymore, he grabbed his keys and headed for his truck. The edge of Blue Falls was visible out his windshield before he had any idea where he was heading. There was something he needed to know, and his brother was just the person to ask.

Ryan strode into the sheriff's department and straight through to Simon's office. He sank into a chair opposite Simon's desk.

"Well, I'm guessing this isn't a 'Hi, big brother, I missed you' visit."

"I need you to find out some information about someone."

"Brooke?"

"No, the guy she ran from." He told Simon what Brooke had told him the day before. "His name is Chris something, and he's some big-time lobbyist in D.C. I want to know how dangerous he might be."

Simon stared at him without speaking for several moments. "You sure you want to go down this road?"

"No matter what she's done or said—or not said—no woman deserves to be that afraid of a man." Despite everything, he'd be hard-pressed not to rip the guy's head off for putting the kind of fear in Brooke that made her feel as if she had to lie.

His anger shifted inside him, dissipating some, making way for more understanding. If he'd felt that trapped, what might he have done in her situation?

"You're in love with her, aren't you?"

His brother, normally the consummate jokester, sounded dead serious. That's when Ryan knew the truth of it, that he did in fact love Brooke Vin…Alder. Whatever her name was, he wanted to be with her. But he had to make sure his family wasn't in any danger first. That Brooke was safe. Then the two of them could start over.

"Yeah, I am."

Simon sighed. "You all are dropping like flies."

A moment passed before Ryan laughed. Despite everything, he laughed hard.

"You should be happy. With Nathan and me out of the way, that clears the way for you with the ladies of Blue Falls."

Simon nodded. "You make an excellent point. You always were the smartest one of us."

He hoped his decision here was a smart one, because he wanted this Chris fella out of Brooke's life for good. He didn't want anything—or anyone—standing in his way when he found the right words to tell her exactly how he felt. That he could no longer imagine his life without her.

Chapter Fourteen

Brooke felt as if her heart had been coated in lead and left to hang heavy and painful in her chest. The lovely sight of the colorful painted bunting couldn't even bring a smile to her face this morning. Maybe it was because she suspected this was the last time she'd walk this familiar path from the bunkhouse to the main house as the sun peeked over the horizon.

She was tired of crying herself to sleep as she had the past two nights, and if she stayed here she feared the tears would never end. Yet again, she was preparing to pack up and start over somewhere else. Only this time she didn't want to leave. But if Ryan didn't come to her today, saying he'd forgiven her and wanted to be with her, she would drive away from Vista Hills and try her best not to fall apart as it faded in the rearview mirror.

The resignation letter weighed down her pocket throughout the morning, and she jerked her gaze to the doorway every time it opened. But it was never Ryan stepping across the threshold, and each time another chunk of her heart broke to pieces.

By the time she'd cleaned up after dinner, she just wanted to get the hard part over with. So she went to Merline's office before she lost her nerve.

"Hey, Brooke. I thought you'd left already."

"No, I needed to give you this." She concentrated on not letting the folded sheet of paper shake as she extended it to Merline.

"What's this?" Merline asked as she took the paper.

"My resignation letter."

Merline shot her a surprised look. "This isn't necessary. I promise, Ryan will come around."

Brooke's lips curved into a sad smile. "I don't think so. And I don't blame him. I wasn't honest with him about my past when he trusted me with his."

Merline tossed the paper aside without reading it. "You did what you thought you had to."

"Why are you so understanding? You didn't even seem surprised when I told you."

"Because I wasn't. When I did your employee paperwork, I found out there was no Brooke Vincent."

Brooke stared at the other woman in disbelief. "And you didn't fire me?"

"You did your job well, and you didn't seem like a criminal. I figured you had to have a good reason, and that when you felt comfortable enough you'd tell me."

"You're too trusting."

Merline shrugged. "If that's the worst I'm ever accused of being, I can live with that."

Trying to grasp everything her boss was telling her, Brooke took a couple of steps and gripped the back of one of the leather chairs facing Merline's desk. "Regardless, I need to go."

"Okay, but I'd like you to stay through the end of the week, give me time to find someone else."

Brooke swallowed, hurt by the idea of someone else in this position she'd unexpectedly come to love. But now that she'd made the decision to leave, she just wanted to go. She suspected Merline was using her guilt to get her to stay, hoping the extra days at the ranch would give Brooke time to change her mind. Maybe time for Ryan to come around. Brooke wasn't going to hold her breath, but she couldn't refuse Merline's request. Not after how kind and understanding the other woman had been.

"Okay, through the end of the week." She paused, watching Merline. "This would be so much easier if you were mad at me for lying."

Merline smiled. "Sorry, can't help you there."

Brooke met the other woman's eyes. "My mom would have really liked you."

"I'm sure I would have liked her as well. After all, she raised a wonderful daughter."

"Thank you, for everything." She turned and left the office before she started blubbering.

She was halfway back to the kitchen when Merline stepped out of her office. "Brooke?"

She turned back around. "Yes?"

"I want you to know that if you do leave, it doesn't have to be forever. You're always welcome here."

Not trusting her voice to perform properly, she gave a little nod and headed out the back door. She might have agreed to stay a few more days, but she still had packing to do. She paused there a moment, leaning back against the side of the house, and pulled her emotions under control.

When she reached the bunkhouse, she set to work packing, knowing that if she stopped, even for a moment, she'd start crying again.

RYAN SAT ON his front porch, a beer in hand, doing something he'd made long practice of avoiding—sorting out his thoughts and feelings.

Simon's investigation into Brooke's past hadn't turned up much that could help him. All he knew was where she'd worked—some swanky D.C. hotel—and that Chris Franklin was a high-powered lobbyist who had a squeaky-clean record. Too squeaky clean, Simon had said.

But he did know what the bastard looked like now. Tall, blond and attractive in that slick business-suit kind of way. It irked him that Brooke had ever been drawn to the man. What did that say about his chances? He was about as similar to Chris Franklin as steak was to tofu.

Approaching footsteps drew his attention and had him standing and walking to the edge of the porch. But it wasn't Brooke who walked out of the dusk, but his mother, instead.

"Good, you're here," she said. "You need to stop pouting and do something about Brooke."

"Hello to you, too."

His mother stopped at the base of the two steps leading up to the porch. "I'm serious, Ryan. She just gave me her resignation letter."

A giant kicked him in the chest. At least that's what it felt like. "She's leaving?"

"Don't sound so surprised. She wanted to leave immediately, but I managed to convince her to stay until the end of the week."

He shifted and braced his palm against one of the porch supports, digging his fingers into the wood. "Is it because of that guy? Did he find her?"

His mom crossed her arms and gave him a hard look. "He's not the guy she's been thinking about." She slowly shook her head. "She's not unlike you, at least how you were until she came here. She can be surrounded by people and still feel totally alone."

"She said that?"

"No, but it's obvious if you just look."

Despite his desire to run to Brooke and beg her not to leave, he stood his ground. "Do you trust her?" He needed reassurance he wasn't being blinded by his feelings for Brooke.

"Yes."

"Why?"

"Because she's in love with my son."

He'd swear the earth shifted under him. Did Brooke love him? He needed to hear it from her, be able to look into her eyes and see the truth there as she said the words. And he realized he needed to say them to her.

And he couldn't let her leave.

No more waiting. No more second-guessing. No more sitting in the shadows examining his feelings under a microscope. It was time for action, to be the man he'd been before that day in the desert.

Brooke closed another box and stacked it on top of the others behind the couch. Another hour's work and she'd be finished, ready to drive away as soon as the week's end came. Well, at least she'd be packed. She didn't think she'd ever be ready to leave this place, these people.

Especially Ryan.

She ran her hands over the table he'd made and debated whether to take it or leave it behind. Did she want to have something to remember him by, or would it be too painful to see it every day?

The sound of her cell phone ringing interrupted her internal debate. She dug in her purse and answered on the third ring, already trying to figure out how to tell Holly that she was running again.

"Hey."

"He's got the girls, Brooke."

Brooke's heart slammed against the confines of her chest as she heard the panic and tears in Holly's voice. "What?"

Holly sniffed. "Chris took the girls. He called and said that he wouldn't hurt them if you came back."

"Oh, my God. Where is he? Did you call the police?"

"He said that I couldn't call the police, that he would just deny everything and they'd believe him."

He really was crazy, even more so than she'd feared.

"Okay, I'll fix this, Holly. I swear to you, the girls will be fine. Where am I supposed to go? Is there a way I can reach him?"

Holly's fragile grip on her emotions crumbled and she sniffed loudly. Her voice shook as she spoke. "All he said was to go where you went hiking, that you'd know what he was talking about."

It took a moment for her spinning mind to fix on the meaning. "Okay."

"Where are they?"

"You can't go there, Holly. I have to do exactly what he says."

"Where?" Holly was more insistent this time. "We have to stay here anyway. Chris calls every half hour and alternates talking to Clay and me, making sure we haven't tried to follow him."

Brooke's hands shook as she tossed a few things in an overnight bag. "Shenandoah National Park. We went hiking there a couple of weeks after we started seeing each other." Back before she knew he was evil in disguise.

Holly didn't hold back her tears. "What do I do, Brooke?"

"Exactly what he says. I'll get them back."

"I hate myself for asking you to do this."

"Don't. This is my fault." She slung the bag over her shoulder and grabbed her purse. "I'm leaving now. Tell him I'm getting there as fast as I can, to not hurt the girls. There's no reason. I'm cooperating."

"Okay."

Brooke ended the call as she slipped into her car and started the engine. She glanced at the bunkhouse one last time before she backed away from it. Once again, she was running away and leaving everything behind. Only this time she was running toward Chris. But she wasn't the same woman who'd fled from him. This time, he wasn't going to win. Once Emma and Caitlyn were safe, she'd figure out a way to get away from Chris again or die trying.

And if he hurt the girls, she'd kill him.

RYAN TREKKED OVER the hills that separated his cabin from the bunkhouse, determined to find the right words that would make Brooke stay. Now that she'd awakened things in him he hadn't known he'd been capable of feeling anymore, he couldn't stand the thought of not being able to see her every day or hold her close at night.

If she'd just stay, they could work through anything.

As he topped the last hill, he saw that the parking space in front of the bunkhouse was empty. Had Brooke left her car at the main house for some reason? But then he noticed that despite the fact the last light of the day was waning, no lights were illuminating the bunkhouse's interior. Fear that she'd left leapt up in him until he remembered Brooke had agreed to stay the rest of the week. And even though she'd told them all lies, his gut told him that her promise to his mom wasn't another one.

But when he reached the bunkhouse and lifted his hand to knock on the door, his certainty faltered. Sticking out of the lock was the key. As his heart sped up, he knocked anyway. When no answer came, he stepped back and considered his options. He walked the short distance to the curve in the road where he could see his parents' house. As he'd feared, Brooke's car wasn't there either.

Afraid of what he'd find, he retraced his steps to the bunkhouse and wrapped his hand around the doorknob. With a deep breath, he turned it and stepped inside, flipping on the ceiling light as he did so.

He exhaled in relief when he saw she hadn't packed up and fled. At least partial relief. She had, in fact, begun packing her belongings in the boxes he'd helped her unpack such a short time ago. An empty box sat atop the kitchen table and he wandered over to it. Inside, on top of a pile of clothes, sat her beauty pageant tiara. He pulled it out and smiled. He'd have to ask to see pictures of that day.

Deciding to wait for her to return from wherever she'd gone, he planted himself in the living room chair where he'd watched her sleep that night when the dark had frightened her. Now he knew what she'd really feared.

With quiet time to think, he let his thoughts wander to a future full of Brooke. Waking up beside her every morning, making love to her, letting her fill up all the empty parts of his life. He loved her, plain and simple. And that's exactly what he was going to say the moment she stepped in the door.

But she didn't appear there, even as night fully fell

on the ranch and one hour stretched into another. He tried calling her on her cell phone but got no answer. An ugly feeling started building in his gut. Something was wrong. His thoughts flew to Chris. Had he somehow found Brooke and waltzed right onto Teague land to steal her back?

If he had, he was going to be sorry when Ryan got his hands on him.

With his nerves and anger warring for dominance, he dialed Simon's number.

"This better be good," Simon said. "I had a hell of a day and just fell asleep."

"Brooke's gone, and I don't think she went willingly."

"Ryan," Simon said in that way of older brothers who thought they were wiser.

"No, something's not right. She left everything behind, and she'd told Mom she stay until the end of the week."

"She's already lied more than once."

"Not this time. Trust me, something is off."

"Okay, I'll do some checking."

"I'll meet you at the station in ten minutes." Ryan hung up before Simon could disagree. With his heart pounding, he ran for his cabin, ignoring the jabs of pain shooting up his damaged leg. When he reached the cabin, he grabbed his truck keys and didn't even pause to lock his door.

It wasn't until he pulled into a parking space in front of the sheriff's office that a sliver of doubt weaseled its way into his brain. What if Simon was right? What if Ryan was once again blind to the truth staring him in the face? Had Brooke played him all along?

He shook his head. No matter what she'd done or said, that thought just didn't ring true. He slid out of the truck and went inside to find Simon at his desk on the phone. Ryan was surprised to see Nathan sitting opposite Simon. No doubt Simon had called him in as backup to deal with their little brother not seeing the truth.

Before he could ask Nathan what he was doing there, Simon hung up the phone. And one look at his older brother's face told him he'd been right.

"What happened?" Ryan asked.

Simon sat back slowly. "Brooke's car was found at the airport in Austin. She's on a flight to D.C."

"She traveling alone?"

Simon nodded, but the tense look tugging at his features told Ryan there was more and it wasn't good.

"I talked with Brooke's sister. She didn't want to say anything at first, but I could tell she knew something. That Chris guy has Holly's two little girls, is holding them until Brooke gives herself up to him. He told her not to tell the police, but she finally broke. I've notified the authorities in Virginia and Shenandoah National Park, where Brooke told Holly she believes he's holding the girls."

The overwhelming need to beat the Chris asshole to within an inch of his life swelled within Ryan. What he'd done to Brooke was bad enough, but to kidnap children to get his way?

"I'll kill that bastard," he said.

"No, you won't," Simon responded. "Even if I have to lock you up until this is all over."

"You can try."

"Stop," Nathan said. "This isn't helping."

Ryan moved to leave.

"Where you think you're going?" Simon asked.

"To find Brooke."

"You'll put those girls in danger if you go off half-cocked."

Ryan stared at his brother and wondered if Simon would respond differently if he wasn't wearing a badge. "You forget I have training. He'll never know I'm there."

Simon sighed and stood. "Well, hell. Looks like I'm going to Virginia, too."

"You don't have to babysit me."

"I'm not. Just going to make sure we all don't have to come visit you in the slammer from now on. I'm not against you giving this guy a good beating, but I'm not letting you kill him."

Ryan didn't argue. The quicker he got out of here without interference from his brothers, the better.

Nathan stood as if he was going, too.

"Nope," Simon said before Ryan could. "I might go along with this clown jetting halfway across the country, but not you. I need you to go back to the ranch and make sure everyone there stays safe in case Chris has other ideas. Plus, Grace would skin me alive if anything happened to you."

Nathan cursed and didn't look happy about being left behind, but he didn't argue.

Ryan turned and stalked out the door. He had to make sure Brooke was safe, that no harm came to her nieces. His fists clenched that she was going back to the man who'd caused her so much fear that she'd run from her life and even her identity.

One way or another, soon she'd never have to worry about Chris Franklin ever again.

Chapter Fifteen

Brooke's stomach was in knots as she made her way toward the northern entrance of Shenandoah National Park. Not breaking the speed limit was the hardest thing she'd ever done, but she couldn't risk being pulled over by the police. The phone call from Chris as she'd walked through the airport had convinced her that if she didn't do exactly what he said, the girls were not safe. And he'd said no cops.

She knew what Chris had planned for her, but she didn't have any choice. Nothing could happen to those precious little girls, and she had to believe that no matter how crazy Chris was he'd honor his promise to release Caitlyn and Emma if he got his way. If not, she'd fight to free them until her dying breath.

Once in the park, she fought off the fatigue brought about by being awake for more than twenty-four hours and drove to the Signal Knob Overlook. She parked there as Chris had instructed. She glanced at her watch and noticed she was a couple of minutes early. Gripping the steering wheel, she prayed that Chris hadn't hurt the girls. She couldn't face a world where she'd be responsible for that. She'd lose her sister, too, and she wouldn't blame Holly for hating her.

At exactly 7:00 a.m., a familiar SUV pulled into the

space next to her. Chris was confident enough that everyone would do exactly what he said that he didn't even try to hide by using a rental car. That chilled her blood more than anything. The very real fact that she might not live to see the end of the day slammed into her, but she didn't let him see that fear. Instead, she got out of her rental car and opened the passenger side of the SUV. Before meeting Chris's gaze, she looked into the back of the SUV but didn't see the girls.

"Where are they?"

"Well, now that's just rude," he said. "No hello or anything?"

She slowly turned to face him. "Where...are...they?"

The mildly affronted look on his face turned dark. "In a safe spot. Now get in."

She hesitated.

"Get in or they might not be safe for long."

For a horrible moment, she feared he had accomplices and that the girls might be held someplace she'd never see them. Feeling she was slipping past the point of no return, she got into the SUV and closed the door. She said nothing as he pulled out of the parking lot and drove farther into the park. After about five minutes, she couldn't stand the silence anymore.

"Where are we going?"

"Somewhere we can be alone. We have a lot of catching up to do."

Bile rose in her throat and it was difficult to swallow it back down. "Why are you doing this?"

"Because you have to be taught a lesson. You misbehave, you get punished."

"But you didn't have to bring the girls into this. They've done nothing to you." Oh, how she hated him, was dying to wrap her hands around his neck and choke the life from him. But if she did that, she would have no idea how to find her nieces. If nothing else good came of this day, she would return the girls to Holly.

"They are, however, very good insurance to make sure you do what you're supposed to. Not that I should have to prod you. After all we've meant to each other, I have to say it hurt to have you run away like that."

She ventured a look at him to see if he was joking. How could someone be that delusional? The fact that he looked as though he believed every word he said sent icy fear through her.

A few minutes later, Chris surprised her by pulling into the Jenkins Gap Overlook. She looked around but saw nothing but a little gray car. Chris parked and cut the engine.

"Get out." Without waiting to see if she obeyed, he got out of the SUV and started walking toward the car.

As Brooke followed, she realized what was happening. Exchanging cars would help throw off any possible police pursuit. Her stomach churned when she thought about how much planning he'd put into this, had likely started the moment he'd discovered she was gone.

She didn't speak as he pulled from the lot and retraced their route back out of the park then down a series of progressively smaller roads. Finally, he turned into a partially overgrown lane that led to a small, 1940s era house. Even before he'd turned off the car, she was flinging open her door and hurrying toward the house. She rushed inside and found the girls tied to two old kitchen chairs, their little mouths gagged. Tear tracks stained their cheeks. Caitlyn's eyes went huge at the sight of her.

"Oh, girls." She started to move toward them, but Chris grabbed her arm to halt her progress. She tried to jerk free, but his grip tightened painfully. "Let me go," she said through clenched teeth.

"You are in no position to give me orders. And you have no right. I'm the wronged party here."

Brooke bit her lip to keep from screaming at him and spitting in his face. "Please let me untie them."

He evidently liked the change in her tone and let her go. She hurried toward them.

"I've done everything you asked," she said. "We need to take them back to their mother."

"We're not going anywhere."

Brooke stopped and turned toward him. "I held up my half of the deal. You said you'd let them go if I came here willingly."

"Oh, I'm letting them go. You and I are just not going anywhere."

She stared at him. "We're miles from anywhere, and they're just little girls."

He shrugged. "They're welcome to stay."

Faced with an impossible choice, Brooke felt like throwing up. Slowly, she turned around at the sound of Emma's wimpers. As she bent to untie their arms and legs, she made her decision. She had to trust the girls could make it out of here, that someone trustworthy would find them. She couldn't let them stay here with Chris. He was too unstable, and she feared what they might see if they stayed. If Chris killed her, he might then turn on them. Praying that she was making the right decision, she removed the gags.

"Aunt Brooke." Emma sobbed and hugged her with all the strength her little arms held.

Brooke gathered both girls in her arms and kissed their heads. "I'm so sorry."

"Where's Mommy?" Emma asked.

"She's waiting for you, sweetie. Everything's okay now." Brooke wiped tears from Emma's red cheeks.

She shifted her attention to Caitlyn. "Are you hurt?"

Caitlyn shook her head and glanced fearfully toward where Chris was moving around on the other side of the room. Brooke pulled her close enough to surreptitiously whisper in her ear.

"When you get outside, I want you to take Emma's hand and you two run as fast as you can."

Caitlyn started to speak, but Brooke squeezed her a bit to cut off the words.

"At the end of the drive, take a left and keep taking bigger and bigger roads until you see someone to call the police, okay?"

Caitlyn nodded. Brooke felt the questions bubbling in her oldest niece, but the girl stayed quiet and trusted her aunt. Brooke didn't make any sudden moves but led the girls toward the door.

"Don't even think about trying to run with them," Chris said, his voice full of the promise of punishment should she go against him.

She didn't respond as she opened the door and ushered the girls outside. "I love you," she said to them.

Fresh tears were streaming down Caitlyn's cheeks this time. She was old enough to grasp that something bad might happen to Brooke but was too young to do anything about it.

Brooke forced a smile. "It's okay. Chris and I are just going to talk." And then she mouthed a single word, "Run."

She watched until they reached the end of the lane then turned and closed the door behind her, determined to do whatever she had to in order to give the girls as much time to escape as possible.

THE LAST THING Ryan wanted to do right now was hang around a police station, but that's exactly what he was being forced to do in some place called Front Royal, Virginia. He and Simon had already told the collection of cops—local, state and federal—all they knew about Brooke and her past. Which wasn't all that much, Ryan had realized as he'd been relaying it.

Now he paced up and down a short hallway next to the station's vending machines.

"You're going to wear out that strip of floor," Simon said from where he stood leaning against the wall.

"I can't sit still." He gestured toward the front of the station. "I should be out there looking for her."

"And where are you going to look?"

"Anywhere, everywhere. I'm sure not going to find her standing in here."

"Just let the authorities do their jobs, Ry. They're following every lead."

Which consisted of a couple on a hiking trail seeing two people fitting Chris and Brooke's descriptions switching vehicles from a dark SUV to a small, gray car.

"He's crazy, Simon! And she's with him." Ryan's heart leapt in his chest when a dark-haired woman stepped around the corner. Brooke.

But it wasn't Brooke. A couple of moments passed before he realized this must be her sister.

"Are you all talking about Brooke?" she asked.

Simon pushed away from the wall. "Yes. You're her sister, aren't you?"

The woman nodded. "Holly." She sniffed and wiped away a tear. "She went after my girls." Holly looked about ready to drop, stretched thin with worry.

Simon and Ryan moved at the same time to help her to a seat. "Are you here alone?" Ryan asked.

"No. Clay, my husband, is on the phone with his parents. But I heard you all talking." She eyed each of them. "You're from the ranch, aren't you?"

"We stand out that much?" Simon asked, trying to lighten the mood by referring to their distinctly cowboy attire.

Holly gave the barest hint of a smile. "A little."

"Have you heard anything new?" Ryan asked her, desperate for some indication that Brooke was okay.

She looked him in the eye then shook her head. "But I know he has Brooke because he stopped calling us to do check-ins."

Some sort of ruckus from the front of the station drew their attention. Ryan looked up in time to see several officers heading toward the front door, where a woman was leading in two little girls. Holly made a strangled sound that was part sob and part cry of relief as she leapt from her chair and raced toward her daughters.

"Thank God," Simon said as Holly wrapped her arms around the girls.

Ryan stood from his crouched position next to Holly's vacated chair. While he was thankful the little girls were safe, he scanned the crowd and the empty doorway beyond. But Brooke wasn't there. A cold knot formed in his stomach.

"I found them out on Baker Hollow Road," said the woman who'd brought in the girls. "They were running, holding hands and had tears streaming down their faces. I think they'd been on their own for hours. They kept saying something about a bad man and their aunt Brooke."

Ryan closed the distance between him and the crowd. Simon caught him and held him back as one of the state police officers leaned down and asked the older girl, "Do you know where your aunt is?"

"In an old white house with that man who took us."

Ryan grew more frustrated as he listened to the girls relay how Brooke had told them to run and how they'd lost count of how many times they'd made turns onto bigger roads until they'd been picked up.

"Don't worry," Simon said beside him. "They'll find her."

"But will they find her in time?" He stalked back toward the vending machines, as crazed as a wild animal forced into the confines of a too-small cage.

"We've got something," one of the officers sitting at a computer said. "Chris Franklin owns a piece of property on Hackney Creek Road."

As several of the officers prepared to leave, Ryan started to follow. Simon grabbed his arm to stop him. Ryan looked hard at his brother. "You're going to want to let go of me, Simon. I'm going, and either you can take me or I can deck you and go without you."

Simon stared right back for several moments. "Fine. But only if you promise me that when we get there, you let these guys do their jobs. You're not seeing straight, and that makes you a danger to Brooke. Let them get her out of there."

Ryan wanted to be the one to rescue her, but if this was the only way to get closer to her he'd agree. If he couldn't rescue her, he'd at least be there to hold her when she was freed from that psychopath. And if the chance to beat in Franklin's face presented itself, so much the better.

As they started to follow the officers out the door, Holly reached up from where she was still holding her daughters and grabbed Ryan's hand. When he met her gaze, tears streamed down her face.

"Please bring my sister back safely."

A knot formed in Ryan's throat as he nodded. "I promise."

EVERY TIME CHRIS made a move toward Brooke, she moved the same amount away from him. Her skin crawled at the idea of having him touch her. Already she'd had to listen to him ramble on for hours about everything she'd done wrong and how he was going to make sure she never left him again. She'd not interrupted, hoping that with each passing minute her nieces were closer to safety.

"You're being rude, Brooke," Chris said as he stalked her as if he were a lion and she his prey. "Is that any way to treat the man you love?"

She backed up slowly, not wanting to prompt him to do something drastic. She scanned the room for something she could use to defend herself because she was not letting him get any closer, no matter that she'd considered going back to him several days ago to protect those she cared about. She couldn't return to the hell of being trapped by him.

"Why did you do this? Why couldn't you just forget me?" she asked.

"I missed you. But of course, you'll have to be punished for running away. I warned you."

He was crazy, completely and utterly crazy.

"Why do you want to be with someone who doesn't want to be with you?" She continued edging away with each step he took, careful not to trip and leave herself any more vulnerable than she already was.

"You just don't know what's good for you. You're confused. I can give you a perfect life."

"You mean the kind of life where you watch me like a hawk and treat me like a prisoner?" She didn't know where the strength to say what she really felt came from, but she grabbed on to it and refused to let go. She was finished letting this man terrorize her.

The falsely pleasant look on his face drained away, leaving behind the angry, controlling man underneath. She wondered how he'd managed to fool so many people, her included. Shouldn't there have been earlier signs that he wasn't stable?

This house hadn't been occupied for a long time, so she was left with little to use as a weapon. Best to keep him talking until she found something or a miracle happened and help arrived.

"Whose house is this?"

"Mine."

That surprised her. She'd figured he'd just scoped out the area until he found an empty, well-hidden place.

"Yes," he continued. "This is my boyhood home. Lovely, isn't it?"

Her forehead scrunched. "You said you grew up in Georgetown." She didn't know why the lie surprised her, but it did.

"That's where I should have grown up, not this pathetic piece of the backwoods." Such contempt stained his words, shame that he'd been common and not exactly wealthy.

She didn't like how the expression on his face changed, as if it was reflecting a deep, bitter anger. Her gaze lit on a carved wooden owl about the size of a football. It wasn't the best weapon imaginable, but it was better than her bare hands. She grabbed it in one swift movement.

Chris's eyes narrowed. "Put that down."

She stood up straight and stared at him hard, no longer cowering. "No. I'm done being afraid of you. I want to leave."

He took another step forward but stopped when she raised the hefty owl. "You can leave, but you're going with me. Back where you belong."

"You're crazy if you think I'm going anywhere with you."

Anger flooded his face, a rising of color and a tensing of his jaw. "You will go, and you won't make a fuss about it."

She gripped the owl more tightly, determined for it not to slip from her grasp. "That's where you're wrong."

A horrible smile stretched across his face. How could she have ever thought him handsome when such darkness slithered beneath the surface? "Look at you, pretending to be all brave. Now, come along before you really make me angry. Your nieces are safe for now, but I bet we could catch up with them."

"You bastard! Stay away from them."

Chris hit his limit of patience. He roared and grabbed a chair then tossed it at her.

Brooke backed up but not fast enough. The chair hit her and caused her to trip over a rag rug. She fell backwards, but miraculously didn't hit her head or lose her grip on the owl. She scrambled to stand, but Chris took the opportunity to tackle her.

"Get off me!" She kicked and writhed and was finally able to take a swing with the owl. She aimed for his head but he shifted and she caught his shoulder instead. Still, she hit him hard enough that his grip loosened and she almost got free.

Chris cursed and slammed into her so hard, pressing her face into the floor, that it was difficult to breathe. It felt as if he'd flattened her lungs inside her body. This time, he'd leave more than psychological scars. She was going to have bruises, whether she lived or not. But she wasn't going to go quietly.

She struggled and screamed, determined to free herself from his clutches. He grasped her hair next to the base of her skull and yanked her head back. Pain shot through her like lightning.

"Don't you ever forget," he yelled next to her ear, "that you are mine!"

Through the roaring in her head, she heard the front door slam open and then the sound of feet rushing into the room. One moment Chris was on top of her, and the next his weight was lifted away. She breathed in huge gulps of air and rolled over.

"Miss Alder, are you okay?" She rolled to her side and blinked until she could focus on the face of a young man in a police uniform.

"The girls?"

"They're fine, at the station with their mother and father."

Brooke closed her eyes and let the tears come.

"What's he doing in here?" she heard someone say and then the scent of pine tickled her nose.

"Brooke?"

It couldn't be, but when she opened her eyes there was Ryan looking at her with fear in his eyes. "Ryan?" Maybe she had hit her head.

The next thing she knew she was in his arms, pressed

close and crying on his shoulder. "I can't believe you're here."

"Of course I'm here."

He said nothing else, but it was enough to make her heart swell with love and hope. But for now, she was satisfied with just holding him.

"Are the girls really okay?"

He pulled back to look into her eyes. "Yes. A lady found them on the side of the road and brought them to the police station. They're with your sister and brother-in-law."

Fresh tears streamed down her cheeks.

"Is this who you've been whoring yourself to?" Chris spat at her.

In a flash, Ryan was on his feet. Before anyone could react, he'd slammed his fist into Chris's jaw. A cop pulled him back and shoved him toward Simon, who'd come into the house at some point.

"Restrain your brother, or I'll have to book him for assault," the cop said.

"He's done," Simon said and steered Ryan back toward Brooke. Simon extended his hand and helped her to her feet.

"Thank you." She shifted her attention to Ryan, who was giving Chris a fierce glare and breathing hard. She lifted her hand to his jaw and forced him to look at her. "He's not worth any more of our attention."

It took him a moment to calm down, but then he nodded. He pulled her into his arms again and kissed her forehead. When he guided her toward the door, she was only too glad to let him. Not even the angry words Chris hurled at them made a dent. Caitlyn and Emma were safe, and she was in Ryan's arms again. It was a miracle considering she'd not been convinced she'd live to see any of them again.

Simon drove them back to the police station, and not once did Ryan let go of her where they sat in the back seat. Even as they headed inside, he kept his arm around her. He didn't break contact until forced to when Holly spotted her and raced forward to take her sister in her arms.

"Oh, Brooke," Holly said through thick tears.

"I'm so sorry, Holly." She looked over Holly's shoulder to where Clay held one of his daughters in each arm. "I'm so sorry," she said to them all.

Holly leaned back and placed her hands on either side of Brooke's face. "This isn't your fault."

"But if it wasn't for me—"

"Stop it," Holly said in a voice that sounded so much like their mother that it startled Brooke into silence. "This is no one's fault but Chris's. You understand me?"

Tears welled in Brooke's eyes. "You don't hate me?"

"No, silly. You're my sister. I love you."

The tears broke free, and they only flowed more freely when Brooke felt little arms go around her waist and leg. She looked down and saw the girls hanging on to her. She lowered to her knees and gathered them close.

"I'm so sorry he scared you," she said, thanking God he'd not done more than that.

Emma was quiet but she hugged Brooke harder. Caitlyn kissed Brooke's cheek. "You're my hero, Aunt Brooke."

Brooke lost it completely and cried into her niece's hair, which despite everything she'd been through that day still smelled like fruity little girl shampoo.

"You're my hero, too," Brooke said. "Both of you.

You were very brave." And they'd no doubt saved her life.

She caught Ryan's gaze over Caitlyn's shoulder and saw an emotion there that made her heart skip. This day just kept producing one miracle after another.

AFTER THEY'D MADE LOVE, Brooke lay in Ryan's arms until she heard his breathing slow into the rhythm of sleep. Then she slid from the bed and slipped on a robe. She crossed to the window and looked out into the night, watched as a few cars drove by on the familiar street. Looking out into the dark didn't scare her anymore because she knew Chris wasn't lurking. He was sitting in a cell somewhere facing kidnapping and assault charges.

She should be sleeping now, but her brain wouldn't settle. She kept reliving everything she'd been through in the past day. The horrible phone call from Holly, the fear that had flown with her back to Virginia, the relief when the girls were safe, the knowledge that she might die, the bone-deep happiness that Holly and Clay didn't hate her, then the seemingly endless questioning by the police after her rescue. Through it all, Ryan had been with her either in spirit or body.

She turned and soaked in the view of Ryan's form. She loved him so much, more than should be possible. Holly had seen it as clearly as their mother would have.

"You love that man, don't you?" she'd asked when she'd caught Brooke watching Ryan and Simon talking across the main area of the police station in Front Royal.

"Yes, I do."

Holly smiled. "No wonder you like that ranch."

Brooke had laughed, and it felt alien after all the fear and anger. Alien, but oh so good.

Careful now not to bump into anything and wake

him, she wandered through her condo, trailing her fingers over all the pieces of her life she'd had to leave behind to flee Chris. Simon had brought them back here but insisted on spending the night in a hotel himself, saying he wanted to stay near the airport since he was flying back to Texas in the morning. The look on his face, however, had told her that he knew how much she and Ryan wanted to be alone. He'd cemented a spot in her heart with that gesture, and she'd lifted on her toes to kiss his cheek.

When she reached the living room, she stopped in the middle and scanned the half-lit furnishings. The connection she'd once had to this place was gone. This wasn't home anymore. She had no idea what her next step would be.

"Brooke?"

She looked back toward her bedroom. "Did I wake you?"

He crossed to where she stood and wrapped his arms around her from behind. "No. But I'd hoped to wake with you still next to me."

She ran her thumb over his fingers clasped in front of her. "I couldn't sleep."

"Do you want to talk about it?"

"About Chris? No. I'm done giving him any thought."

Ryan turned her to face him. "Then what's bothering you?"

"I can't stop thinking about how scared the girls were, how what I did could have led to someone else getting hurt."

"But it didn't."

She looked up at him, so close. "But it could have. I can't help thinking that even though it's over, I still feel lost."

He caressed her jaw then gestured to their surroundings. "It's because this isn't you anymore."

She marveled at how perceptive he was, more like Merline than Brooke had realized.

"How can you all ever trust me again after the lies I told? Your family could have been in the line of fire."

"Let's get one thing straight," he said. "How upset I was before, forget it."

"No, you were right to be angry."

Ryan slid his hands to either side of her face and gently forced her to meet his gaze. "Listen to me. Stop punishing yourself. You did what you had to do. We all understand that."

"But—"

He cut her off with a kiss, one she was powerless to resist. When he broke the contact, he ran his thumb along her bottom lip.

"Stop looking back, and really see what's in front of you. We all love you. *I* love you."

"You…"

He smiled. "That's right, I said it. I love you, Brooke Alder."

She bit her lip at the sound of those words combined with her real name, her real self. And all thoughts of ever living apart from this man fled. The smile that started quickly consumed her.

"I love you, too."

"Good, because I wouldn't help just anyone pack all this stuff up. Or drive the truck it's going to take to get it all back to Texas."

She laughed then kissed him again, long and very, very thoroughly.

"So, you're going to help me pack, huh?"

He swept her off her feet and into his arms. "Maybe

tomorrow," he said as he retraced his steps to the bedroom.

Yes, tomorrow was soon enough. Tonight, she had to show Ryan Teague just how much she loved him.

Chapter Sixteen

"Going to be a gorgeous sunset," Grace said as she drove up the road leading into the ranch.

Brooke looked out her window at how the sun had painted the western horizon a stunning palette of orange, red and pink.

"That, it is." Despite the fact she'd lived almost all of her life back East, now she couldn't imagine spending the rest of her days anywhere but the Hill Country. Anywhere but this ranch.

Every day, she found herself more a part of this place and the lives of the people around her. Case in point, she'd just finished working with Keri Mehler of the Mehlerhaus Bakery on a reception for a local artist at Merline's gallery. Unhindered by the fear of being discovered, she'd had a wonderful time getting to know Keri better, as well as a lot of other Blue Falls residents. She was free to be herself—a mixture of the person she used to be in West Virginia then D.C. and the woman she'd become since coming to the ranch.

She returned her attention to the road in front of them and noticed a slice of unexpected color rising above the live oaks and cedars. Leaning forward, she asked, "What is that?" When Grace didn't answer, she looked at her friend and saw she was trying to hide a smile.

Grace steered around the last bend, and Brooke gasped. A tethered hot air balloon sat in the field to the right of the barn. "What in the world?" she asked as Grace parked.

"You'll have to ask Ryan." Grace winked and got out of the car.

Brooke slid out of the car slowly, still unable to believe her eyes. The yellow and blue panels of the balloon reminded her of the fields of wildflowers through which she and Ryan had hiked a few days before.

He approached her from the direction of the balloon, and she moved to meet him while still marveling at the sight of the balloon. "What is this?"

"They tell me it's called a hot air balloon."

She swatted him on the shoulder. "But why is it here?"

He smiled as he took her in his arms. "A little birdie might have told me you'd always wanted to take a ride in one."

It took her a moment, but then she remembered a snippet of conversation right after she'd arrived at the ranch. "That birdie named Merline?"

"Could be." He nodded back at the balloon. "You like it?"

"Are you kidding? I love it."

"Well, if you like that, I have something else you're going to like even better." He looked past her and nodded.

Curious, she turned. Her eyes filled with tears, happy ones, at the sight before her.

"Aunt Brooke!" Emma broke away from her sister and mother and ran toward Brooke.

Laughing and crying at the same time, she leaned down and scooped the little ball of energy into her arms.

She kissed Emma on the cheek, and then Caitlyn. After the intense fear of losing them, she didn't think she'd be able to hug and kiss and love them enough. There would be no stopping her from being the aunt who spoiled them rotten with gifts.

Holly caught up with her daughters and joined in the group hug.

"How? When?" Brooke couldn't manage to speak much beyond single-word questions.

"Ryan invited us down for a surprise visit," her sister said. "I had to see this new home of yours for myself."

After several minutes of catching up and more hugs, Holly pulled her daughters to her side. "Let's give Aunt Brooke some space. She's got a balloon ride to take."

Brooke glanced at the balloon, so magical in the waning light of day, but it was nothing compared to having her family with her.

"Go on before it gets dark," Holly said. "We'll be here waiting for you."

"I have to prepare dinner. I'm already behind."

Holly grabbed Brooke's hand and squeezed it. "For once, do what your sister tells you." She leaned closer so only Brooke could hear. "Get in that balloon with that sexy man."

Brooke smiled wide. "You're married, sis."

"But I ain't blind. Besides," she said as she nodded toward the barn, "I think the rest of this clan is trying to convert Clay from a dairy farmer into a cowboy. I might be all for the idea if he also converts to tight jeans."

Brooke eyed the entrance to the barn and saw Nathan, Simon and Hank giving Clay the grand tour. She laughed and hugged her sister close. "I'm so glad you're here. I've missed you so much."

"Me, too. Now go."

Brooke went, her insides vibrating with happiness. Ryan opened a little door in the side of the balloon's basket and escorted her in. She was surprised that the balloonist didn't get in with them.

"Don't worry, it's tethered," Ryan said. "I think I can manage the distance we're going up."

The girls waved at them as they started ascending, and they waved back. Their little girl giggles carried up to them as they cleared the trees. When she looked out toward the west, not only could she see the last blazing streaks of the sunset but also the twinkling lights of Blue Falls down in the valley.

"It's so beautiful," she said.

"You're beautiful."

When she looked at Ryan, he wasn't paying the sunset or the lights any mind. His attention was firmly focused on her, and it made her go warm all over.

"Thank you for this," she said. "And for bringing my family here."

"Well, I didn't have much choice. Your sister said that if she wasn't here when I asked you, she'd have my head."

Brooke's breath caught as Ryan pulled something out of his pocket and held her gaze as he slowly lowered himself to one knee.

"Brooke Alder, would you make me the happiest man in Texas and be my wife?"

"Yes," she whispered. Then more strongly, she said it again. "Yes!"

Ryan slid the diamond onto her finger then stood and pulled her into his arms. "Good thing you said yes, or I was going to keep us up here until you changed your mind."

"I can think of worse things." She lifted onto her toes and touched her lips to his.

"Me, too," he said before he kissed her like she hoped he would keep kissing her for the rest of their days.

"Is that a yes?" Simon yelled up from the ground.

She looked over the side of the basket and saw that all the Teagues had gathered and Clay now had his arm around Holly. Brooke extended the hand with the shiny new ring on it. "It's a yes!"

A great whoop went up from the collection of people on the ground, so many people she loved. Her family, both of blood and of the heart. The girls jumped up and down in a circle holding hands.

"They look happy," Ryan said beside her.

She looked up at him and hoped all the love she felt was reflected on her face. "Not as happy as me."

He caressed her cheek. "Or me."

And then her angel-carving, furniture-making, fiddle-playing, balloon-flying cowboy kissed her until she no longer needed the balloon to float on air.

* * * * *

HEART & HOME

COMING NEXT MONTH
AVAILABLE APRIL 10, 2012

#1397 BABY'S FIRST HOMECOMING
Mustang Valley
Cathy McDavid
A year after Sierra Powell gave her baby up
for adoption, little Jamie was returned to her.
Determined to make a new life for both of
them, she returns to Mustang Valley to reunite
with her estranged family. But she doesn't
expect to run into Clay Duvall, a former enemy
of the Powells...and the secret father of her son.

#1398 THE MARSHAL'S PRIZE
Undercover Heroes
Rebecca Winters

#1399 TAMED BY A TEXAN
Hill Country Heroes
Tanya Michaels

#1400 THE BABY DILEMMA
Safe Harbor Medical
Jacqueline Diamond

REQUEST YOUR FREE BOOKS!
2 FREE NOVELS PLUS 2 FREE GIFTS!

❤ Harlequin®

American ★ Romance®

LOVE, HOME & HAPPINESS

YES! Please send me 2 FREE Harlequin® American Romance® novels and my 2 FREE gifts (gifts are worth about $10). After receiving them, if I don't wish to receive any more books, I can return the shipping statement marked "cancel." If I don't cancel, I will receive 4 brand-new novels every month and be billed just $4.49 per book in the U.S. or $5.24 per book in Canada. That's a saving of at least 14% off the cover price! It's quite a bargain! Shipping and handling is just 50¢ per book in the U.S. and 75¢ per book in Canada.* I understand that accepting the 2 free books and gifts places me under no obligation to buy anything. I can always return a shipment and cancel at any time. Even if I never buy another book, the two free books and gifts are mine to keep forever.

154/354 HDN FEP2

Name _____
(PLEASE PRINT)

Address _____ Apt. #

City _____ State/Prov. _____ Zip/Postal Code

Signature (if under 18, a parent or guardian must sign)

Mail to the Reader Service:
IN U.S.A.: P.O. Box 1867, Buffalo, NY 14240-1867
IN CANADA: P.O. Box 609, Fort Erie, Ontario L2A 5X3

Not valid for current subscribers to Harlequin American Romance books.

Want to try two free books from another line?
Call 1-800-873-8635 or visit www.ReaderService.com.

* Terms and prices subject to change without notice. Prices do not include applicable taxes. Sales tax applicable in N.Y. Canadian residents will be charged applicable taxes. Offer not valid in Quebec. This offer is limited to one order per household. All orders subject to credit approval. Credit or debit balances in a customer's account(s) may be offset by any other outstanding balance owed by or to the customer. Please allow 4 to 6 weeks for delivery. Offer available while quantities last.

Your Privacy—The Reader Service is committed to protecting your privacy. Our Privacy Policy is available online at www.ReaderService.com or upon request from the Reader Service.

We make a portion of our mailing list available to reputable third parties that offer products we believe may interest you. If you prefer that we not exchange your name with third parties, or if you wish to clarify or modify your communication preferences, please visit us at www.ReaderService.com/consumerschoice or write to us at Reader Service Preference Service, P.O. Box 9062, Buffalo, NY 14269. Include your complete name and address.

HAR11B

Taft Bowman knew he'd ruined any chance he'd had for happiness with Laura Pendleton when he drove her away years ago...and into the arms of another man, thousands of miles away. Now she was back, a widow with two small children...and despite himself, he was starting to believe in second chances.

Harlequin Special® Edition® presents a new installment in USA TODAY *bestselling author RaeAnne Thayne's miniseries,* THE COWBOYS OF COLD CREEK.

Enjoy a sneak peek of
A COLD CREEK REUNION

Available April 2012 from Harlequin® Special Edition®

A younger woman stood there, and from this distance he had only a strange impression, as though she was somehow standing on an island of calm amid the chaos of the scene, the flashing lights of the emergency vehicles, shouts between his crew members, the excited buzz of the crowd.

And then the woman turned and he just about tripped over a snaking fire hose somebody shouldn't have left there.

Laura.

He froze, and for the first time in fifteen years as a firefighter, he forgot about the incident, his mission, just what the hell he was doing here.

Laura.

Ten years. He hadn't seen her in all that time, since the week before their wedding when she had given him back his ring and left town. Not just town. She had left the whole damn country, as if she couldn't run far enough to get away from him.

Some part of him desperately wanted to think he had made some kind of mistake. It couldn't be her. That was just some other slender woman with a long sweep of honey-blond hair and big, blue, unforgettable eyes. But no. It was definitely Laura. Sweet and lovely.

Not his.

He was going to have to go over there and talk to her. He didn't want to. He wanted to stand there and pretend he hadn't seen her. But he was the fire chief. He couldn't hide out just because he had a painful history with the daughter of the property owner.

Sometimes he hated his job.

Will Taft and Laura be able to make the years recede...or is the gulf between them too broad to ever cross?

Find out in
A COLD CREEK REUNION
Available April 2012 from Harlequin® Special Edition®
wherever books are sold.

Celebrate the 30th anniversary
of Harlequin® Special Edition® with a bonus story
included in each Special Edition® book in April!